# He came to a dead stop and swallowed hard.

Every bit of what she was wearing was borrowed. Yet somehow his new assistant managed to look like a fashion model for an outdoor company. Suddenly, he realized that Dylan was correct. Libby Parkhurst had a kick-ass body.

Libby's eyes snapped open, her expression guarded. "Good morning," she said.

He hated the guilt that choked him. "Libby, I—"

She held up a hand, stopping his instinctive words. "I don't want to talk about it."

They stared at each other for several long seconds. He forced himself to zero in on basics.

He slid one backpack off his shoulder. "I need to make sure the straps are adjusted correctly for you." Without asking, he stepped behind her and helped settle the pack into position. With a few quick tugs, he was satisfied. Finally, he moved in front of her and fiddled with the strap at her chest.

Libby made some kind of squawk or gasp. It was only then he realized his fingers were practically caressing her breasts. He stepped back quickly. "I'm sure you can manage the waistband," he muttered.

"Uh-huh." She kept her head down while she fiddled with the plastic locking mechanism. After a moment, she stared off into the woods. "I'm good."

\* \* \*

***How to Sleep with the Boss***
is part of The Kavanaghs of Silver Glen series:
In the mountains of North Carolina, one family
discovers that wealth means nothing without love.

Dear Reader,

One of my very first books was called *Tent for Two*. It's been out of print for years, but it was the only book I ever wrote where the hero and heroine spent a night alone in the woods.

In *How to Sleep with the Boss*, I had great fun putting my Park Avenue heiress (who has lost all her money) in a setting where she has to depend on the hero to keep her safe. I also enjoyed watching Patrick Kavanagh fall in love with a woman who is so completely wrong for him, and yet so right.

Life can be surprising and wonderful when we occasionally step outside our comfort zones. Take a chance on new experiences this year!

And as always, thanks so much for reading...

*Janice Maynard* ☺

# HOW TO SLEEP WITH THE BOSS

## JANICE MAYNARD

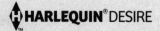

Recycling programs
for this product may
not exist in your area.

ISBN-13: 978-0-373-73441-2

How to Sleep with the Boss

Copyright © 2016 by Janice Maynard

Never Too Late
Copyright © 2006 by Harlequin Books S.A.
Brenda Jackson is acknowledged as the author of this work.

**Printed in U.S.A.**

HARLEQUIN®
www.Harlequin.com

# CONTENTS

*USA TODAY* bestselling author **Janice Maynard** knew she loved books and writing by the time she was eight years old. But it took multiple rejections and many years of trying before she sold her first three novels. After teaching kindergarten and second grade for a number of years, Janice turned in her lesson plan book and began writing full-time. Since then she has sold over thirty-five books and novellas. Janice lives in east Tennessee with her husband, Charles. They love hiking, traveling and spending time with family.

Hearing from readers is one of the best perks of the job!

You can connect with Janice at twitter.com/janicemaynard, facebook.com/janicemaynardreaderpage, wattpad.com/user/janicemaynard, and instagram.com/janicemaynard.

### Books by Janice Maynard

**Harlequin Desire**

*The Kavanaghs of Silver Glen*

*A Not-So-Innocent Seduction*
*Baby for Keeps*
*Christmas in the Billionaire's Bed*
*Twins on the Way*
*Second Chance with the Billionaire*
*How to Sleep with the Boss*

Visit the Author Profile page at Harlequin.com, or janicemaynard.com, for more titles!

# HOW TO SLEEP WITH THE BOSS

## Janice Maynard

For Caroline and Anna: beautiful daughters,
dear friends, exceptional women...

# One

"I want you to push me to my limits. So I can prove to you that I can handle it."

Patrick stared across his paper-cluttered desk at the woman seated opposite him. Libby Parkhurst was not someone you would pick out of a crowd. Mousy brown hair, ordinary features and clothes at least one size too big for her slender frame added up to an unfortunate adjective. *Forgettable.*

Except for those eyes. Green. Moss, maybe. Not emerald. Emerald was too brilliant, too sharp. Libby's green eyes were the quiet, soothing shade of a summer forest.

Patrick cleared his throat, absolutely sure his companion hadn't intended her remark to sound provocative. Why would she? Patrick was nothing more to her than a family friend and a prospective employer. After all, Libby's mother had been his mother's best friend for decades.

"I appreciate your willingness to step outside your comfort zone, Libby," he said. "But I think we both know this job is not for you. You don't understand what it involves." Patrick's second in command, Charlise, was about to commence six months of maternity leave. Patrick needed a replacement ASAP. Because he had dawdled in filling the spot, his mother, Maeve Kavanagh, had rushed in to supply an interviewee.

Libby sat up straighter, her hands clenched in her lap, her expression earnest and maybe a tad desperate. "I do," she said firmly. "Maeve described the position in detail. All I'm asking is that you run me through the paces before I have to welcome the first group."

Patrick's business, Silver Reflections, provided a quiet, soothing setting for professionals experiencing burnout, but also offered team-building activities for high-level management executives. Ropes courses, hiking, overnight survival treks. The experience was sometimes grueling and always demanding.

The fill-in assistant would be involved in every aspect of running Silver Reflections. While Patrick applauded Libby's determination, he had serious doubts about her ability to handle the physical aspects of the job.

"Libby..." He sighed, caught between his instincts about filling the position and his obligation to play nice.

His unwanted guest leaned forward, gripping the edge of his desk with both hands, her knuckles white. "I need this job, Patrick. You know I do."

Libby had him there. He'd witnessed in painful detail what the past year had been like for her—as had most of the country, thanks to the tabloids. First, Libby's father had been sent to prison for tax fraud to the tune of several million. Then eight weeks ago, after months of being hounded by the press and forced to adopt a lifestyle far below her usual standards, Libby's emotionally fragile mother had committed suicide.

Quite simply, in the blink of an eye, Libby Parkhurst

had gone from being a sheltered heiress to a woman with virtually no resources. Her debutante education had qualified her to host her father's dinner parties when her mother was unable or unwilling to do so. But twenty-three-year-old Libby had no practical experience, no résumé and no money.

"You won't like it." He was running out of socially acceptable ways to say he didn't want her for the job.

Libby's chin lifted. She sat back in her chair, her spine straight. The disappointment in her gaze told him she anticipated his rejection. "I know your mother made you interview me," she said.

"I'm far past the age where my mother calls the shots in my life." It was only partly a lie. Maeve Kavanagh wielded maternal guilt like a sharp-edged sword.

"I don't have anything left to lose," Libby said quietly. "No home. No family. No trust fund. It's all gone. For the first time in my life, I'm going to have to stand on my own two feet. I'm willing and able to do that. But I need someone to give me a chance."

*Damn it.* Her dignified bravery tugged at heartstrings he hadn't tuned in ages. Why was Libby Parkhurst his problem? What was his mother thinking?

Outside his window, the late-January trees were barren and gray. Winter still had a firm hold on this corner of western North Carolina. It would be at least eight weeks before the first high-adventure group arrived. In the meantime, Libby would surely be able to handle the hotel aspects of the job. Taking reservations. Checking in guests. Making sure that all reasonable requests were accommodated.

But even if he split Charlise's job and gave Libby the less onerous part, he'd still be stuck looking for someone who could handle the outdoor stuff. Where was he going to find a candidate with the right qualifications willing to work temporarily and part-time?

If this had been an emotional standoff, Libby would have won. She never blinked as she looked at him with all the entreaty of a puppy begging to be fed. He decided to try a different tack. "Our clients are high-end," he said. "I need someone who can dress the part."

Though her cheeks flushed, Libby stood her ground. "I've planned and overseen social events in a penthouse apartment overlooking Central Park. I think I can handle the fashion requirements."

He eyed her frumpy clothing and lifted a brow...not saying a word.

For the first time, Libby lowered her gaze. "I suppose I hadn't realized how much I've come to rely on the disguise," she muttered. "I've dodged reporters for so long, my bag-lady routine has become second nature."

Now he was the one who fidgeted. His unspoken criticism had wounded her. He felt the taste of shame. And an urgent need to make her smile. "A trial period only," he said, conceding defeat. "I make no promises."

Libby's jaw dropped. "You'll hire me?"

The joy in her damp green eyes was his undoing. "Temporarily," he emphasized. "Charlise will be leaving in two weeks. In the meantime, she can show you how we run things here at the retreat center. When the weather gets a bit warmer, you and I will do a dry run with some of the outdoor activities. By the end of February, we'll see how things are going."

He had known "of" Libby for most of his life, though their paths seldom crossed. Patrick was thirty...Libby seven years younger. The last time he remembered seeing her was when Maeve had taken Patrick and his brothers to New York to see a hockey game. They had stopped by the Parkhurst home to say hello.

Libby had been a shy redheaded girl with braces and a ponytail. Patrick had been too cool at the time to do more than nod in her direction.

And now here they were.

Libby smiled at him, her radiance taking him by surprise. "You won't be sorry, I swear."

How had he thought she was plain? To conceal his surprise, he bent his head and scratched a series of numbers on a slip of paper. Sliding it across the desk, he made his tone flat...professional. "Here's the salary. You can start Monday."

When she saw the amount, Libby's chin wobbled.

He frowned. "It's not a lot, but I think it's fair."

She bit her lip. "Of course it's fair. I was just thinking about how much money my family used to spend."

"Is it hard?" he asked quietly. "Having to scrimp after a lifetime of luxury?"

"Yes." She tucked the paper in her pocket. "But not in the way you think. The difficult part has been finding out how little I knew about the real world. My parents sheltered me...spoiled me. I barely knew how to cook or how much a gallon of milk cost. I guess you could say I was basically useless."

Feeling his neck get hot, he reached for her hand, squeezing her fingers before releasing her. Something about Libby brought out his protective instincts. "No one is useless, Libby. You've had a hell of a year. I'm very sorry about your mother."

She grimaced, her expression stark. "Thank you. I suppose I should tell you it wasn't entirely a surprise. I'd been taking her back and forth to therapy sessions for weeks. She tried the suicide thing twice after my father's trial. I don't know if it was being without him that tormented her or the fact that she was no longer welcome in her social set, but either way, her pain was stronger than her need to be with me."

"Suicide never makes sense. I'm sure your mother loved you."

"Thank you for the vote of support."

Patrick was impressed. Libby had every right to feel sorry for herself. Many women in her situation would latch onto the first available meal ticket…anything to maintain appearances and hang on to the lifestyle of a wealthy, pampered young socialite.

Libby, though, was doing her best to be independent.

"My mother thinks the world of you, Libby. I think she always wanted a daughter."

"I don't know what I would have done without her."

Silence fell suddenly. Both of them knew that the only reason Patrick had agreed to interview Libby was because Maeve Kavanagh had insisted. Still, Patrick wasn't going to go back on his word. Not now.

It wouldn't take long for Libby to realize that she wasn't cut out for the rigorous physical challenges that awaited her at Silver Reflections. Where Charlise had been an athlete and outdoorswoman for most of her life, Libby was a pale, fragile flower, guaranteed to wilt under pressure.

Over the next two weeks, Patrick had cause to doubt his initial assessment. Libby dived into learning her new responsibilities with gusto. She and Charlise bonded almost immediately, despite the fact that they had little in common, or so it seemed.

Charlise raved about Libby's natural gifts for hospitality. And the fact that Libby was smart and focused and had little trouble learning the computer system and a host of other things Charlise considered vital to running Silver Reflections.

On the second Friday morning Libby was on his payroll,

Patrick cornered Charlise in her office and shut the door. "Well," he said, leaning against the wall. "Is she going to be able to handle it?"

Charlise reclined in her swivel chair, her amply rounded belly a match for her almost palpable aura of contentment. "The girl's a natural. We've already had four clients who have rebooked for future dates based on their interactions with Libby. I can honestly say that I'm going to be able to walk away from here without a single qualm."

"And the outdoor component?"

Charlise's glow dimmed. "Well, maybe a tiny qualm."

"It's one thing to run this place like a hotel. But you and I both know we work like dogs when we take a group out in the woods."

"True. But Libby has enthusiasm. That goes a long way."

"Up until a year ago I imagine she was enjoying pedicures at pricey Park Avenue salons. Hobnobbing with Fortune 500 executives who worked with her dad. It's a good bet she never had anyone steal her lunch money."

Charlise gave him a loaded look. "You're a Kavanagh, Patrick. Born with a silver spoon and everything that goes with it. Silver Reflections is your baby, but you could walk away from it tomorrow and never have to work another day in your life."

"Fair enough." He scratched his chin. "There's one other problem. I told Libby that she would have to dress the part if she planned to work here. But she's still wearing her deliberately frumpy skirts and sweaters. Is that some kind of declaration of independence? Did I make a faux pas in bringing up her clothing?"

"Oh, you poor, deluded man."

"Why does no one around here treat me with respect?"

Charlise ignored his question. "Your mother offered to buy Libby a suitable wardrobe, but your newest employee is independent to say the least. She's waiting to go shopping until this afternoon when she gets her first paycheck."

"Oh, hell."

"Exactly."

"Wait a minute," he said. "Why can't she wear the clothes she had when her dad went to prison? I'll bet she owned an entire couture wardrobe."

"She did," Charlise said, her expression sober. "And she sold all those designer items to pay for her mom's treatments. Apparently the sum total of what she owns can now fit into two suitcases."

Patrick seldom felt guilty about his life choices. He did his best to live by a code of honor Maeve had instilled in all her boys. Do the right thing. Be kind. Never let ambition trump human relationships.

He had hired Libby. Now it was time to let her know she had his support.

Libby was in heaven. After months of wallowing in uncertainty and despair, now having a concrete reason to get up every morning brought her something she hadn't found in a long time...confidence and peace.

For whatever reason, Patrick Kavanagh had made himself scarce during Libby's first two weeks. He'd left the training and orientation entirely up to Charlise. Which meant Libby didn't constantly have to be looking over her shoulder. With Charlise, Libby felt relaxed and comfortable.

They had hit it off immediately. So much so that Libby experienced a pang of regret to know Charlise wouldn't be coming back after today. Just before five, Libby went to Charlise's office holding a small package wrapped in blue paper printed with tiny airplanes. Charlise and her accountant husband were looking forward to welcoming a fat and healthy baby boy.

Libby knocked at the open door. "I wanted to give you this before you go."

Charlise looked up from her chore of packing personal items. Her eyes were shiny with tears. "You didn't have to do that."

"I wanted to. You've been so patient with me, and I appreciate it. Are you okay? Is anything wrong?"

Charlise reached for a tissue and blew her nose. "No. I don't know why I'm so emotional. I'm very excited about the baby, and I want to stay at home with him, but I love Silver Reflections. It's hard to imagine not coming here every day."

"I'll do my best to keep things running smoothly while you're gone."

"No doubts on that score. You're a smart cookie, Libby. I feel completely confident about leaving things in your hands."

"I hope you'll bring the baby to see us when the weather is nice."

"You can count on it." She opened the gift slowly, taking care not to rip the paper. "Oh, Libby, this is beautiful. But it must have been way too expensive."

Libby grimaced. She had been very honest with Charlise about her current financial situation. "It's an antique of sorts. A family friend gave it to my parents when I was born, engraved with the initial *L*. When I heard you say were going to name the baby Lander, after your father, I knew I wanted you to have it."

"But you've kept it all this time. Despite everything that's happened. It must have special meaning."

When Libby looked at the silver baby cup and bowl and spoon, her heart squeezed. "It does. It did. I think I held on to the set as a reminder of happier times. But the truth is, I don't need it anymore. I'm looking toward the future. It will make me feel good to know your little boy is using it."

Charlise hugged Libby tightly. "I'll treasure it."

Libby glanced at her watch. "I need to let you get out of here, but may I ask you one more thing before you go?"

"Of course."

"How did you get this job working with Patrick?"

"My husband and Patrick's brother Aidan are good friends. When Patrick put out the word that he was starting Silver Reflections, Aidan hooked us up."

"And the high-adventure stuff?"

Charlise shrugged. "I've always been a tomboy. Climbing trees. Racing go-karts. Broke both arms and legs before I made it to college. At different times, thank goodness."

"Good grief." Libby thought about her own cocoon-like adolescence. "Do you really think I can handle the team building and physical challenges in the outdoors?"

The other woman paused, her hand hovering over a potted begonia. "Let me put it this way…" She picked up the plant and put it in a box. "I think you'll be fine as long as you believe in yourself."

"What does that mean?"

"I've heard you talk about Patrick. He intimidates you."

"Well, I—" Libby stopped short, unable to come up with a believable lie. "Yes."

"Don't let him. He may come across as tough and intense at times, but underneath it all, he's a pussycat."

A broad-shouldered masculine frame filled the doorway. "I think I've just been insulted."

# Two

Libby was mortified to be caught discussing her new boss. Charlise only laughed.

Patrick went to the pregnant woman and kissed her cheek, placing his hand lightly on her belly. "Tell that husband of yours to call me the minute you go to the hospital. And let me know if either of you needs anything... anything at all."

Charlise got all misty-eyed again. "Thanks, boss."

"It won't be the same without you," he said.

"Stop that or you'll make me cry again. Libby knows everything I know. She's exactly who you need... I swear."

Patrick smiled. "I believe you." He turned to Libby. "How about dinner tonight? I've tried to stay out of the way while Charlise showed you the ropes, but I think it would be good for the two of us to get to know each other better. What do you say?"

Libby felt herself flush from her toes to the top of her head. Not that this was a date. It wasn't. Not even close.

But Patrick Kavanagh was an imposing specimen. Despite his comfortably elegant appearance at the hotel, she had the distinct sense that beneath the dark suits and crisp ties lurked someone who was very much a man's man.

The kind of guy who made a woman's toes curl with just one look from his intense blue-gray eyes. He was tall and lean and had a headful of unruly black hair. The glossy, dark strands needed a comb. Or maybe the attention of a lover's fingers.

Her heart thumped hard, even as her stomach tumbled in a free fall. "That would be nice," she said. *Great.* Now she sounded like a child going to a tea party at her grandma's house.

Charlise picked up her purse and a small box. Patrick hefted the larger carton and followed her out of the room, leaving Libby to trail behind. Outside, the air was crisp and cold. She shivered and pulled her sweater more tightly across her chest.

Patrick stowed Charlise's things and hugged her. The affection between the two was palpable. Libby wondered what Charlise's husband was like. Obviously, he must be quite a guy if he let his wife work day after day with the darkly handsome Patrick Kavanagh.

Charlise eased behind the wheel, closed the car door and motioned for Libby to come closer. Patrick's phone had rung, and he was deep in conversation with whoever was on the other end.

Libby rested a hand in the open window and leaned down. "You're going to freeze," she said.

The pregnant woman lowered her voice. "Don't let him ride roughshod over you. You're almost too nice sometimes. Stand up to him if the occasion warrants it."

"Why would I do that? He's the boss."

Charlise grinned and started the engine. "Because he's too damned arrogant for his own good. All the Kavanagh men are. They're outrageously sexy, too, but we women have to draw a line in the sand. Trust me, Libby. Alpha males are like dangerous animals. They can smell fear. You need to project confidence even when you don't feel it."

"Now you're scaring me," Libby said, only half joking.

"I've known Patrick a long time. He admires grit and determination. You'll win his respect. I have no doubt. And don't worry about the survival training. What's the worst that could happen?"

Libby watched the car drive away, burdened with an inescapable feeling that her only friend in the world was leaving her behind in the scary forest. When she turned around, the lights from the main lodge of Silver Reflections cast a warm glow against the gathering darkness.

Since Patrick was still tied up on the phone, she went back to Charlise's office—now Libby's—and printed out the staff directory. She planned to study it this weekend. Facts and figures about everyone from the housekeeping staff to the guy who kept the internet up and running. Even at an executive retreat center famed for creating an atmosphere of solitude and introspection, no one at the level of these guests was going to be happy without a connection to the outside world.

Patrick found her twenty minutes later. "You ready to go? I guess it makes sense to take two cars."

Silver Reflections was tucked away in the mountains ten miles outside of town. In the complete opposite direction stood the magnificent Silver Beeches Lodge. Perched on a mountaintop overlooking Silver Glen, it was owned and operated by Maeve Kavanagh and her eldest son, Liam. Libby hesitated before answering, having second thoughts. "I'm sure you must have better things to do with your weekend. I'm not really dressed for dinner out."

Patrick's eyes darkened with a hint of displeasure. "If it

will make you feel better, I'll include these hours in your paycheck. And dinner doesn't have to be fancy. We can go to the Silver Dollar."

Patrick's brother, Dylan, owned a popular watering hole in town. The saloon was definitely low-key. Certainly Libby's clothing would not make her stand out there. "All right," she said, realizing for the first time that Patrick's invitation was more like an order. "I'll meet you there."

During the twenty-minute drive, she had time to calm her nerves. She already had the job. Patrick wasn't going to fire her yet. All she had to do was stick it out until they did some of the outdoor stuff, and she could prove to him that she was adaptable and confident in the face of challenges.

That pep talk carried her all the way into the parking lot of the Silver Dollar. The requisite pickup trucks were definitely in evidence, but they were interspersed with Lexus and Mercedes and the occasional fancy sports car.

Libby had visited this corner of North Carolina a time or two over the years with her mother. Silver Glen was a high-end tourist town with a nod to alpine flavor and an unspoken guarantee that the paparazzi were not allowed. It wasn't unusual to see movie stars and famous musicians wandering the streets in jeans and baseball caps.

Most of them eventually showed up at the Silver Dollar, where the beer was cold, the Angus burgers prime and the crowd comfortably raucous. Libby hovered on the porch, waiting for Patrick to arrive. The noise and color and atmosphere were worlds away from her native habitat in Manhattan, but she loved it here.

At Maeve's urging, Libby had given up the New York apartment she could scarcely afford and had come to North Carolina for a new start. Truth be told, her native habitat was feeling more and more distant every day.

Patrick strolled into view, jingling his car keys. "Let's

grab a table," he said. "I called Dylan and told him we were on our way."

In no time, they were seated. Libby ordered a Coke... Patrick, an imported ale. Dylan stopped by to say hello. The smiling, very handsome bar owner was the second oldest in the seven-boy Kavanagh lineup. Patrick was the second youngest.

Patrick waved a hand at Libby. "Do you remember Libby Parkhurst? She's going to fill in for part of Charlise's maternity leave."

Dylan shook Libby's hand. "I do remember you." He sobered. "I was sorry to hear about your mother. We have an apartment upstairs here at the Silver Dollar. I'd be happy to give it to you rent-free until you've had a chance to get back on your feet."

Libby narrowed her gaze. "Did your mother guilt you into making me an offer?"

Dylan's neck turned red. "Why would you say that? Can't a man do something nice without getting an inquisition?"

Libby stared from one brother to the other. Apparently, down-on-her-luck Libby had become the family *project*. "If you're positive it won't be an imposition," she said slowly. "I'm taking up a very nice guest room at Maeve's fancy hotel, so I'm sure she'd rather have me here."

Dylan shook his head. "Maeve is delighted to have you *anywhere*. Trust me. But she thought you'd like some privacy."

Patrick studied Libby's face as she pondered the implications of living above the bar. It was hardly what she was used to...but then again, he had no idea what her life had been like after the tax guys had swooped in and claimed their due.

Dylan wandered away to deal with a bar-related problem, and on impulse, Patrick asked the question on his mind. "Will you tell me about this past year? Where you've been? How things unfolded? Sometimes it helps to talk to a neutral third party."

Libby sipped her Coke, her gaze on the crowd. Friday nights were always popular at the Silver Dollar. He studied her profile. She had a stubborn chin, but everything else about her was soft and feminine. He would bet money that after one night in the woods, Libby was going to admit she was in over her head.

When she looked at him, those beautiful eyes gave him a jolt—awareness laced with the tiniest bit of sexual interest. He shut down that idea quickly. Maeve would have his head on a platter if he messed with her protégé. And besides, Libby wasn't his type. Not at all.

Libby's lips curved in a rueful half smile. "It was frightening and traumatic and definitely educational. Fortunately, my mother had a few stocks and bonds that were in her name only. We managed to find an apartment we could afford, but it was pretty dismal. I wanted to go out and look for work, but she insisted she needed me close. I think losing the buffer of wealth and privilege made her feel painfully vulnerable."

"What about your father?"

"We had some minimal contact with him. But Mama and I both felt betrayed, so we didn't go out of our way to visit. I suppose that makes me sound hard and selfish."

Patrick shook his head. "Not at all. A man's duty is to care for his family. Your father deceived you, broke your trust and failed to provide for you. It's understandable that you have issues."

She stared at him. "You speak from experience, don't you? My mother told me about what happened years ago."

Patrick hadn't expected her to be so quick on the uptake. Now he was rather sorry he'd raised the subject. His own father, Reggie Kavanagh, had been determined to find the lost silver mine that had made the first Kavanaghs in North Carolina extremely wealthy. Reggie had spent months, years…looking, always looking.

His obsession cost him his family.

"I was just a little kid," Patrick said. "My brother Liam has the worst memories. But yeah…I understand. My mother had every right to be bitter and angry, but somehow she pulled herself together and kept tabs on seven boys."

Libby paled, her eyes haunted. "I wish I could say the same. But not all of us are as strong as Maeve."

He cursed inwardly. He hadn't meant to sound critical of Libby's mother. "My mother wasn't left destitute."

"True. But she's made of tough stock. Mama was never really a strong person, even in the best of times."

"I'm sorry, Libby."

Her lips twisted, her eyes bleak. "We can't choose our families."

In an instant he saw that this job idea was laden with emotional peril for Libby Parkhurst. When it became glaringly obvious that she couldn't handle the physically demanding nature of Charlise's role as his assistant, Libby would be crushed. Surely it would be better to find that out sooner than later. Then she could move on and look for employment more suited to her skill set. Libby was smart and organized and intuitive.

There was a place for her out there somewhere. Just not at Silver Reflections.

He drummed his fingers on the table. "I looked at the weather forecast. We're due to have a warm spell in a couple of days."

"I saw that, too. Maeve says you almost always get an early taste of spring here in the mountains, even if it doesn't last long."

"She's right. And in light of that, why don't you and

I go ahead and take an overnight trip, so I can show you what's involved."

Libby went from wistful to deer in the headlights. "You mean now?"

"Yes. We could head out Monday morning and be back Tuesday afternoon." Part of him felt guilty for pushing her, but they had to get past this hurdle so she could see the truth.

He saw her throat move as she swallowed. "I don't have any outdoor gear."

"Mom can cover you there. And my sisters-in-law can loan you some stuff, too. No sense in buying anything now."

"Because you think I'll fail."

She stared him down, but he wasn't going to sugarcoat it. "I think there is a good chance you'll discover that working for me isn't what you really want."

"You've made up your mind already, haven't you?" He was surprised to see that she had a temper.

"No." Was he being entirely honest? "I promised you a trial run. I've merely moved up the timetable, thanks to the weather."

Libby's gaze skewered him. "Do I need a list from you, or will your mother know everything I need?"

"I'll email you the list, but Mom has a pretty good idea."

Libby stood up abruptly. "I don't think I'm that hungry, after all. Thank you for the Coke, *Mr. Kavanagh*. If you'll excuse me, it sounds like I have a lot to do this weekend."

And with that, she turned her back on him and walked out of the room.

Dylan commandeered the chair Libby had vacated, his broad smirk designed to be irritating. "I haven't seen you crash and burn in a long time, baby brother. What did you say to make her so mad?"

"It wasn't a date," Patrick said, his voice curt. "Mind your own damned business."

"She could do better than you, no doubt. Great body, I'm guessing, even though her clothes are a tad on the eccentric side. Excellent bone structure. Upper-crust accent. And those eyes… Hell, if I weren't a married man, I'd try my luck."

Patrick reined in his temper, well aware that Dylan was yanking his chain. "That's not funny."

"Seriously. What did you say to run her off?"

"It's complicated."

"I've got all night."

Patrick stared at him. "If you must know, Mom shoved her down my throat as a replacement for Charlise. Libby can handle the retreat center details, but there is no way in hell she's going to be able to do all the outdoor, back-country stuff. When I hired her, she asked me to give her a chance to prove herself. I merely pointed out that the weather's going to be warm the first of the week, so we might as well go for it."

"And that made her mad?"

"Well, she might possibly have assumed that I expect her to fail."

"Smart lady."

"How am I the bad guy here? I run a multilayered business. I can't afford to babysit Mom's misfits."

Dylan's expression went from amused to horrified in the space of an instant.

Libby's soft, well-modulated voice broke the deadly silence. "I left my sweater. Sorry to interrupt."

And then she was gone. Again.

Patrick swallowed hard. "Did she hear what I said?"

Dylan winced. "Yeah. Sorry. I didn't have time to warn you. I didn't see her coming."

"Well, that's just peachy."

The waitress appeared, notepad in hand, to take Patrick's order. "What'll you have?" she asked.

Dylan shook his head in regret. "Bring us a couple of burgers, all the way. My baby brother needs some cheering up. It's gonna be a long night."

# Three

Not since the wretched aftermath of her father's arrest had Libby felt so small and so humiliated. She'd thought Patrick liked her…that he was pleased with her work to date. But in truth, Libby had been foisted on him, and he resented her intrusion.

Her chest hurt, almost as if someone had actually sucker punched her. When she made it back to her room on the third floor of Maeve's luxurious hotel, Libby threw herself on the bed and cried. Then she cussed awhile and cried some more. Part of her never wanted to see Patrick Kavanagh again. The other part wanted to make him ashamed for having doubted her. She wanted to be the best damn outdoorswoman he had ever seen.

But since that was highly unlikely to be the actual scenario come Monday, perhaps the best course was to explain to Maeve that the job hadn't worked out.

There would be questions, of course, lots of them. And although there might be other jobs in Silver Glen, perhaps as a shop assistant making minimum wage, it would be difficult to find a place to live on that kind of paycheck. She owed Maeve a huge debt of gratitude. Not for anything in the world did she want to seem ungrateful.

Which left Libby neatly boxed into an untenable situation.

Saturday morning she awoke with puffy eyes and a headache. It was only after her third cup of coffee that she even began to feel normal. Breakfast was out of the question. She felt too raw, too bruised. There was no reason to think Patrick would be anywhere near the Silver Beeches Lodge, but she wasn't taking any chances.

After showering and dressing in jeans and a baggy sweater, Libby sent a text to Maeve, asking her to drop by when she had a minute. In the meantime, Libby studied her paycheck. She had planned to buy the first pieces of her professional wardrobe this weekend. But if she was going to be fired Tuesday night, it made no sense to pay for clothes she might not need.

One step at a time.

When Maeve knocked on the door around eleven, Libby took a deep breath and let her in.

Maeve hugged her immediately. "I want to hear all about the job," she said, beaming. "I saw Charlise in town Wednesday, and she said you were amazing."

Libby managed a weak chuckle. "Charlise is being kind."

The two of them sat down in armchairs beside the gas log fireplace. Although now Libby could barely afford the soap in the bathroom, the upscale accommodations were familiar in their amenities. Growing up, she had traveled widely with her parents.

Maeve smoothed a nonexistent wrinkle from her neatly pressed black slacks. Wearing a matching blazer and a fuchsia silk blouse, she looked far younger than her age, certainly too young to have seven adult sons. "So tell me," she said. "How do you like working for Patrick?"

"Well…" Libby hesitated. She'd never been a good liar, so she had to tiptoe through this minefield. "I've spent most of my time with Charlise. But everyone on the staff speaks very highly of your son."

"But what do *you* think? He's a good-looking boy, isn't he?"

At last Libby's smile felt genuine. "Yes, ma'am. Patrick is a hottie."

"I know I'm prejudiced, but I think all my sons turned out extremely well."

"I know you're proud, and rightfully so."

"Five of them already married off to wonderful women. I think I'm doing pretty well."

*Uh-oh.* "Maeve, surely you're not thinking about playing matchmaker. That would be extremely uncomfortable for me."

Maeve's face fell. "What do you mean?"

"I'm starting my life from scratch," Libby said. "I have to know I can be an independent person. Although I was too naive to realize it at the time, my parents sheltered me and coddled me. I want to learn how to negotiate the world on my own. Romance is way down the list. And besides, even I know it's not a good idea to mix business with pleasure."

If a mature, extremely sophisticated woman could sulk, that's what Maeve did. "I thought you'd appreciate my help."

"I *do*," Libby said, leaning forward and speaking earnestly. "You looked out for me at the lowest point in my life. You helped me through Mama's death and took me in. I'll never be able to thank you enough. But at some point, you have to let me make my own choices, my own mistakes. Otherwise, I'll never be sure I can survive on my own."

"I suppose you're right. Is that why you wanted to see me this morning? To tell me to butt out?"

Libby grinned, relieved that Maeve had not taken offense. "No. Actually, I need your help in rounding up some hiking gear. Patrick wants to take advantage of the warm weather coming up to teach me what I'll need to know for the team-building, outdoor-adventure expeditions."

"So soon? Those usually don't begin until early April."

"I think he wants to be sure I can handle the physical part of the job." Libby spoke calmly, but inwardly she cringed, Patrick's words still ringing in her ears. *I can't afford to babysit Mom's misfits.*

Maeve stared at her intently. Almost as if she could tell something else was going on. "Write down all your sizes," she said. "I'll gather everything you need and meet you here tomorrow around one."

"I really appreciate it."

Maeve stood. "I have a lunch appointment, so I need to run. You'll get through this, Libby. I know how strong you are."

"Mentally or physically?"

"They go hand in hand. You may surprise yourself this week, my dear. And you may surprise Patrick, as well."

Patrick's mood hovered somewhere between injured grizzly and teething toddler. He was ashamed of himself for letting his aggravation make him say something stupid. But damn it, he'd been talking to his brother…letting off steam. He didn't go around kicking puppies and plucking the heads off flowers.

He was a nice guy.

Unfortunately for him, he could think of at least one person who didn't think so.

During the weekend, he gathered the equipment he would need to put Libby through her paces. Normally, he and Charlise shared the load: supervising the employees who organized the meals, interacting with the executives, teaching skills, coaching the group through difficult activities.

But Charlise was not only accustomed to being outdoors, she also had a great deal of experience in living off the land.

Libby didn't. It was as simple as that.

Patrick tried to juggle things in his mind, ways for him to take over some of Charlise's duties so that Libby could handle a lighter load. But that would only postpone the inevitable. This first experience had to play out as closely as possible to the real thing, so Libby would understand fully what was involved and what she could expect.

By Monday morning, his mood hadn't improved. He'd gone through his checklist on autopilot, but of course, he'd had to cover Charlise's prep, as well. He arrived at Silver Reflections several minutes before eight so he would have some time to mentally gear up for the day's events.

Libby's car was already parked in the small wooded lot adjacent to the building. It was an old-model Mercedes with a badly dented fender. Suddenly Patrick remembered where he had seen the car before. Liam's wife had driven it a couple of years ago until a teenage kid backed into her at the gas station.

Liam had decided it wasn't worth fixing and bought Zoe a brand-new mommy van. The damaged car had been in Liam's garage the last time Patrick saw it. Apparently, Maeve wasn't opposed to getting the whole family in the act when it came to her "rescue Libby" plan.

Patrick headed inside, greeted the receptionist with an absent wave and holed up in his office. Taking a deep breath, he leaned a hip against his desk, pulled his phone out and sent a text.

We'll leave at nine if that works for you...

Libby's response was immediate: I'll be ready.

Meet me out front.

He wondered if Libby was nervous. Surely so. But he knew her well enough already to be damned sure she wouldn't let the nerves show.

At 8:55 he hefted all their gear and headed outside, only to get his first shock of the day. Libby leaned against a tree, head back, eyes closed. On the ground at her feet lay a waterproof jacket. From head to toe, she was outfitted appropriately. Sturdy boots, lightweight quick-dry pants, a white shirt made of the same fabric and an aluminum hiking pole. He came do a dead stop and swallowed hard.

Every bit of what she was wearing was borrowed. Yet inexplicably she managed to look like a model for some weird amalgam of *Vogue* and L.L.Bean. The clothing fit her better than anything she had worn so far in his employ. Suddenly, he realized that Dylan was correct. Libby Parkhurst had a kick-ass body.

When he shifted from one foot to the other, he dislodged a piece of gravel. Libby's eyes snapped open, her expression guarded. "Good morning," she said.

He hated the guilt that choked him. "Libby, I—"

She held up a hand. "I don't want to talk about it."

They stared at each other for several long seconds. He couldn't get a read on her emotions. So he shoved aside the memory of her face in Dylan's bar and forced himself to zero in on basics.

"Three things," he said tersely. "The moment you feel

anything on your foot begin to rub, we stop and deal with it. A major key to hiking in the mountains is taking care of your feet. Blisters can be incapacitating. Understood?"

"Yes, sir."

Her smart-ass tone was designed to annoy him, but he didn't take the bait. "Secondly, if I'm walking too fast for you, you have to say so. There's no need to play the martyr."

"Understood."

"Lastly, you have to drink water. All day. All the time. Women don't like the idea of peeing in the woods, so they tend to get dehydrated. That's also dangerous."

The look on Libby's face was priceless. "Got it," she mumbled.

"Am I being too blunt?" he asked.

She gnawed her lip. "No. I suppose I hadn't thought through all the ramifications."

"That's what this trip is about."

He slid one of two backpacks off his shoulder. "I need to make sure the straps are adjusted correctly for you." Without asking, he stepped behind her and helped settled the pack into position. With a few quick tugs, he was satisfied. Finally, he moved in front of her and fiddled with the strap at her chest.

Libby made some kind of squawk or gasp. It was only then that he realized his fingers were practically caressing her breasts. He stepped back quickly. "I'm sure you can manage the waistband," he muttered.

"Uh-huh." She kept her head down while she dealt with the plastic locking mechanism. After a moment, she stared off into the woods. "I'm good."

"Then follow me."

Libby had taken yoga classes from the time she was fourteen, although during the past year, she'd had to keep up the discipline on her own. She was limber and more than moderately fit. But Patrick's punishing pace had her gasping for breath by the third mile.

His legs were longer than hers. He knew the rhythm of walking over rough terrain. And she was pretty sure he had loaded her pack with concrete blocks. But if Charlise could do this, so could she.

Fortunately, the boots Maeve had found for Libby were extremely comfortable and already broken in. Given Patrick's warning, Libby paid close attention to her feet. So far, no sign of problems.

It helped that the view from behind was entertaining. Patrick's tight butt and long legs ate up the miles. She had long since given up estimating how far they had come or what time it was. Since her phone was turned off to save the battery, she was dependent upon Patrick's knowledge of the forest to get them where they needed to go.

At one point when her legs ached and her lungs burned, she shouted out a request. "Water, please." That was more acceptable to her pride than admitting she couldn't keep up.

Patrick had a fancy water-thingy that rested inside his pack and allowed him to suck from a thin hose that protruded. Not the kind of item a person borrows. So he had tucked plastic pouches of water for Libby in the side pockets of her pack. She opened one and took a long, satisfying gulp. It took everything she had not to ask how much farther it was to their destination.

The two of them were completely alone…miles away from the nearest human. The wind soughed through the trees. Birds tweeted. The peace and solitude were beautifully soothing. But a chasm existed between Patrick and her. At the moment, she had no desire to breach it.

As forecasted, the warming trend had arrived with a

vengeance. Temperatures must already be in the upper sixties, because Libby's skin was damp with perspiration.

Patrick hadn't said a word during their stop. He merely stood in silence, his attention focused on the scenery. The trail had ascended a small ridgeline, and through a break in the trees, they could see the town of Silver Glen in the distance.

"I'm good," she said, stashing the water container. "Lead on."

Her body hurt and her lungs hurt, but eventually, she fell into a rhythm that was almost natural. *One foot in front of the other. Zen-like state of being. Embrace the now.*

It almost worked.

When they stopped for lunch, she could have sworn it was at least seven in the evening. But the sun was still high in the sky. Patrick had a more sophisticated standard for trail food than she had anticipated. Perhaps a certain level of cuisine was de rigueur for his Fortune 500 clients. Instead of the peanut butter and jelly she had expected, they enjoyed baked-ham sandwiches on homemade bread.

When the meal was done and Patrick shoved their minimal trash into his pack, she finally asked a question. "What do you do if you have someone who can't handle the hiking?"

He zipped his pack and shouldered it. "Companies apply to come to Silver Reflections. We have a long waiting list. Most of the elite businesses institute some kind of wellness programs beforehand. They'll include weight loss, stress management, regular exercise…that kind of thing. So by the time they come to North Carolina, most of the participants are mentally and physically prepared for the adventure rather than dreading it."

"I see." But she didn't really. Patrick was already walking, so she stumbled after him. "But what about people that aren't prepared? Do they make them come anyway?"

Patrick didn't turn around, but his voice carried. "A lot of top corporations are beginning to realize the importance of physical well-being for their employees as a means to increase the bottom line. If an executive has a physical limitation, then of course he or she isn't forced to come. But if an otherwise physically capable person chooses not to attend to his or her health and fitness, then it might be a sign that a top-shelf promotion isn't in the cards."

With that, the conversation ended. Patrick was walking as quickly as ever, making it look easy. Maybe Libby had slipped into the numb stage, or maybe she was actually getting used to this, but her aches and pains had receded. Perhaps this was the "runner's high" people talked about. Endorphins at work, masking the physical discomfort.

At long last, Patrick stopped and took off his pack to stretch. Libby followed suit, looking around curiously. It was obvious they had reached their destination. Patrick stood on the edge of a large clearing. The area was mostly flat. About thirty feet away, a narrow creek slid and tumbled over rocks, the sound of the water as soothing as the prospect of wetting tired feet in the chilly brook.

Patrick shot her a look, clearly assessing her physical state. "This is base camp."

"There's not much to it," she blurted out.

"Were you expecting a five-star hotel?"

His sarcasm on top of everything else made her angry, but she didn't want him to get the best of her. So she kept her mouth shut. If he wanted her to talk, he was going to have to initiate the conversation.

Somehow, it seemed almost obscene to be at odds with another human in the midst of such surroundings. Though it would be several more weeks until the new green of spring began to make its way through the sun-kissed glades, even now the forest was beautiful.

She dropped her pack and managed not to whimper.

Though it galled her to admit it, maybe Patrick was right. Maybe this job was not for her. It was one thing to come out here alone with him. But in the midst of an "official" expedition, Libby would be expected to pull her weight. Her new boss wouldn't be free to coach her if she got in over her head.

He knelt and began pulling things from his pack. "The first thing Charlise usually does is put up our tents. I'll be teaching the group how to do theirs."

"Okay." How hard could it be? The one-man tents were small.

"First you'll want the ground cover. It's the thing that's silver on one side and red on the other. Silver side up to preserve body heat."

Libby was a fast learner. And she was determined to acquit herself well. "Got it."

Patrick pointed. "Leader tents go over there." He stood, hands on hips, while she struggled to spread the ground tarps and smooth them out.

Next came the actual tents. Claustrophobically small and vulnerably thin, they were actually not that difficult to set up. Lightweight poles snapped together in pieces and threaded through a nylon sleeve from one corner of the tent to the opposite side. Repeat once, and it was done. The only thing left was to secure the four corners to the ground with plastic stakes.

All in all, not a bad effort for her first time. Even Patrick seemed reluctantly impressed. He handed her a rolled-up bundle that was about eighteen inches wide. "Look for a valve on one corner. It's not difficult to blow up. And it won't look like much when you're done. But having this pad underneath your upper body and hips makes for a much more comfortable night."

He was right. Even when she inflated the thin *mat-*

*tress*, it didn't seem like much of a cushion. But she wasn't about to say so.

To give Patrick his due, he didn't go out of his way to make her feel nervous or clumsy. Still, having someone watch while she learned new skills was stressful.

At last, both tents were up, pads and sleeping bags inside. The full realization that she and Patrick were going to spend the night together hit her hard. No television. No computers. Nothing at all for a distraction. He was gorgeous and unavailable. She was lonely and susceptible.

Nevertheless, the job was what she needed. Not the man. She couldn't let him see that she was seriously attracted to him. Cool and casual was the plan.

She stood and arched her back. "What next?"

# Four

Patrick hadn't expected much from a young, pampered, New York socialite. But perhaps he was going to have to eat his words. During the morning, he had set an intentionally punishing pace as they made their way through the woods. Libby stayed on his heels and never once complained.

Was it the past year that had made her resilient, or was she naturally spunky and stubborn? That would remain to be seen.

He glanced at his watch. Even with this current spring-like spell, it was still February, which meant far less daylight than in two months when he traditionally scheduled his first team-building treks. Kneeling, he pulled a small camp stove from his pack. "I'll show you how to use this," he said. "The chef at the retreat center has a couple of part-time assistants who prepare our camping meals the day before."

"I assumed the execs would have to cook for themselves. Isn't that part of the outdoor experience?"

"In theory, yes. But so far, we've only done short trips... two days, one night. So our time frame is limited. Since we want them to do a lot of other activities, we preprepare the food and all they have to do is warm it up. We don't spend too much time on meals."

Once Libby had mastered the stove, she glanced up at him. "Surely you don't expect the entire group to use something this small."

"No. I have a group of local guys who come along to carry the food, extra stoves and extra water."

He stared at her, disconcerted by feelings that caught him unawares. He was *enjoying* himself. Libby was a very soothing person to be around. When she stood up, he walked away, ostensibly picking up some fallen limbs that had littered the campsite.

Grappling with an unexpected attraction, he cursed inwardly. With Charlise, he never felt like he was interacting with a woman. He treated her the same way he did his brothers. Charlise was almost part of his family. While he was delighted that she and her husband were so happy about the upcoming birth, he would be lying if he didn't admit he was feeling a little bit sorry for himself. Silver Reflections had been going so well. He had honed these outdoor events down to the finest detail. Then Charlise had to go and get pregnant. And his mother had saddled him with Libby. A remarkably appealing woman who'd already managed to get under his skin.

What was he going to do about it? Nothing. It would be a really bad idea to get involved personally with his mother's beloved Libby. Not only that, but with Charlise out of commission, he had no choice but to work twice as hard. And ignore his libido.

Surely he could be excused for being a little grumpy.

Libby called out to him. "What now?"

He turned around and caught her rolling her shoulders. She'd be sore tomorrow. Backpacking used a set of muscles most people didn't employ on a daily basis.

"I'll show you how we string our packs up in the trees," he said.

"Excuse me?"

He sighed, the look of befuddlement on her face the sign of an outdoor newbie. "Once we set up camp, we won't be hauling our backpacks everywhere. We'll use this as home base and range around the area."

"Why can't we leave the packs in our tents?"

"Bears," he said simply.

Up until that point, Libby had done an admirable job keeping her cool, but now she paled. "What do you mean, *bears*?"

"Black bears have an incredible sense of smell. And they're omnivorous. Anytime we're away from camp— and at night when we're sleeping—we'll hang our packs from a high tree limb to discourage unwanted visitors. Don't keep any food in your tent at all, not even a pack of crackers or scented lip balm or toothpaste."

"I washed my hair with apple shampoo this morning." Her expression was priceless.

"Not to worry. I should have told you. But the scent won't be strong enough by the end of the day to make a difference."

"Easy for you to say," she grumbled as she glanced over her shoulder, perhaps expecting a bear to lumber into sight any moment.

Patrick unearthed a packet of nylon rope. "There will be plenty of tall men around to do this part, but it never hurts to gain a new life skill. Watch me, and then you can try."

"If you say so."

He found a rock that was maybe four inches around

and tied it to the end of the rope. "Stand back," he said. Fortunately for his male pride, his first shot sailed over the branch. He reached for the rock again and removed it. "Now all you have to do is attach one end to your pack, send it up, and tie it off." When Libby seemed skeptical, he laughed, his good humor restored for the moment. "Never mind. I won't make you practice this right now. We have better things to do."

"Like what?"

He grabbed a couple of water pouches and a zippered nylon case, then hefted both packs toward the treetops, securing them. "I'm going to show you where I teach the groups how to rappel."

Libby's expression was dubious. "Does Charlise do the rappelling thing?"

It was the first time she had seemed at all reluctant to approach something new. "No. Not usually. So if you don't want to try it, you can watch me. But I do want you to get a feel for the whole range of activities we offer. C'mon… it's not far."

As they passed the two tents, neatly in place for the up-coming night, he felt his pulse thud. He'd never thought of camping out as sexual or even sensual. When he spent time with a woman, it was in fine restaurants or at the theater. Perhaps later on soft sheets in her bedroom. But certainly not when both parties were sweaty—and without a luxurious bathroom at hand.

He stumbled. Damn it. Libby was messing with his head.

The large rock outcropping was barely half a mile away. He strode automatically, only slowing down when he realized that Libby was lagging behind. When she caught up, he moved on without speaking.

Though she had been cooperative and pleasant all day, his inadvertent insult from Friday hung between them like a cloud. He would have to address it sooner or later, whether she liked it or not.

When they arrived at their destination, he unzipped the bag and pulled out a mass of tightly woven mesh straps. "Sometimes, if we have women along, I might ask you to help them get into their gear. If a female seems extremely modest or uneasy, it can be difficult for me or one of the guys to help with the harness…you know…too much touching."

Libby nodded. "I understand."

She stared at him intently as he prepared the equipment. Something about her steady regard made the back of his neck tingle. "I'm going to go around the side of that ridge and come out on top," he said. "That cliff is only about thirty feet high, but it looks really far off the ground when you're standing up there, particularly if you've never done anything like this before."

"I can imagine."

He tossed her a thin ground cloth to sit on. "Feel free to relax while I get up there. And you don't have to worry about ticks or other bugs. It's still too early for a lot of creepy crawlies."

Libby *hadn't* been worrying about creepy crawlies, but she was now. Ick. Her legs itched already from the power of suggestion.

If her companion had been any man other than Patrick Kavanagh, she might have assumed he was showing off. He could have explained how the rappelling worked without a demonstration. Maybe he just liked doing it. It was a sure bet he didn't have any interest in impressing her.

Without Libby to slow him down, he appeared at the top of the small cliff in no time at all. She shaded her eyes and watched as he secured himself to a nearby tree. He checked all of his connections and waved. Then, looking like an extremely handsome and nimble spiderish super-hero, he stepped backward off the rock shelf and danced his way to the bottom.

His skill was striking.

Something about a man so physically powerful and at ease with his body was very appealing. For a moment, she thought about other, more primal things he might do exceedingly well...but no. She wouldn't go there.

Once before when she was young and immature, she'd fallen under the spell of a magnetic, powerful man—with disastrous results. History would not be repeating itself. She was older now, old enough to be tempted. But sex and romance were off the table. Keeping this job had to be her focus.

The demonstration took some time. Once Patrick reached the bottom, he had to go back to the top and untie his ropes.

Finally, he reappeared, striding toward her. She handed him his water. He dropped down beside her, barely breathing heavily, and took long gulps. Already, the sun was sliding lower in the sky, and a chill began to linger in the shadows.

Libby pulled her knees to her chest and linked her arms around her legs. "That was pretty cool. Have you always been fond of the outdoors?"

Patrick wiped the back of his arm across his forehead. "Would you be surprised to know that I worked in advertising for several years in Chicago?"

She gaped at him. "Seriously?"

His smile was self-mocking. "Yes. I loved the competitive atmosphere—stealing big accounts, coming up with the next great ad campaign. Brainstorming with smart, focused, energetic colleagues. It was a great environment for a young man."

She snorted. "You're still young."

"Well, you know what I mean."

"Then what changed?"

He shrugged. "I missed the mountains. I missed Silver Glen. I didn't know how deeply this place was imprinted on my DNA until I left. So one day, I turned in my notice, and I came home."

"And started Silver Reflections."

"It took a couple of years, but yeah…it's been a pretty exciting time."

"So who's the real Patrick Kavanagh? The man I just watched scramble down a cliff? Or the sophisticated guy who roams the halls of his übersuccessful, private, luxurious executive getaway?"

His quick grin startled her. "Wow, Libby…was that a compliment?" Without waiting for an answer to his teasing question, he continued. "Both, I guess. Without the time in Chicago, I doubt I would have understood the needs of the type A men and women who eat, sleep and breathe work. I was one of them…at least for a few years. But I realized my life was missing balance. For me, the balance is here. So if I can offer rest and recovery to other people, then I'm satisfied."

"And your personal life?" Oops. That popped out uncensored. "Never mind. I don't want to know."

He chuckled but kept silent.

They were sitting so close, she could smell his warm skin and the hint of whatever soap he had used that morning. Not aftershave. That would be the equivalent of inviting bears to munch on his toes. Even mentally joking about it gave her a shiver of unease.

Not long from now, it was going to get dark. Very dark. Her nemesis, Patrick Kavanagh, was the only person metaphorically standing between her and the wildness of nature.

To keep her mind off the upcoming night, she asked another question. "Do you have any regrets?"

"Yes," he said quietly. "I'm sorry I said something so stupid and unkind, and I'm sorry you heard it."

She flushed, though in the fading light, maybe he couldn't see. "I told you I don't want to talk about it. You're entitled to your opinion."

He touched her knee. Briefly. As if to establish some kind of connection. "I admire the hell out of you, Libby. I didn't mean what I said on Friday night. My mother is one of the best people I know. Her instincts are always spot-on. Her compassion and genuine love for people have influenced my brothers and me more than we'll ever know."

"You called me a misfit."

Patrick cursed beneath his breath. "Don't remind me, damn it. I'm sorry. It was a crappy thing to do."

"I think the reason it hurt me was because it's the truth."

Patrick leaped to his feet and dragged her with him, his hands on her shoulders. "Don't be ridiculous."

He looked down at her, his jaw tight. He was big and strong and absolutely confident in everything he did. With the five-inch difference in their heights, it would be easy to rest her head on his shoulder. She was tired of being strong all the time. She was tired of not knowing who she was anymore. And she really wanted the luxury of having a man like Patrick in her life. But survival trumped romance right now.

"You've been a trouper today," he said quietly.

"But I'm not Charlise."

One beat of silence passed. Then two.

"No. You're not. But that doesn't mean you aren't capable in your own way."

He wasn't dodging the truth. Where she came from they called that *damning with faint praise*.

"I can learn," she said firmly. Was she trying to convince Patrick or herself?

His small grin curled her toes in her boots. "I know that. And I'm sorry I hurt your feelings. I'm not usually such an animal. Please forgive me."

She wasn't sure who was more surprised when he bent his head and kissed her. When either or both of them should have pulled away, some spark of longing kept them together. At least it felt like longing on her part. She didn't know *what* Patrick was thinking.

His lips pressed hers firmly, his tongue teasing ever so gently, asking permission to slide inside her mouth and destroy her with the taste of him. Her arms went around his neck. Clinging. Her body leaned into his. Yearning. It had been well over a year since she had been kissed. Echoes of past mistakes set off alarms, but she ignored them.

The moment of rash insanity set her senses on fire, helping her forget that she'd walked through her own kind of purgatory. It felt so good to be held. So safe. So warm. She trembled in his embrace.

"Patrick..." She whispered his name, not wanting to stop, but knowing they were surely going to regret whatever madness had overtaken them.

He jerked as if he had been shot. Staggered backward. "Libby. Hell..."

The exclamation encompassed mortification. Shock. Regret.

It was the last one that stung, despite knowing that keeping distance between them was for the best.

She managed a smile, though it cost her. "We'd better get back to camp. I'm starving, and it's going to be dark soon."

His apology should have erased the friction, yet they faced each other almost as adversaries.

He nodded, his expression brusque. "You're right."

This time, following him through the forest came naturally. No matter the strained atmosphere between them, in this environment, she trusted him implicitly to take them wherever they needed to go.

Dinner was homemade vegetable soup warmed on the camp stove. The chef had made the entrée and added fresh Italian rolls to go with it. While Libby tended to the relatively foolproof job of preparing the meal, Patrick started a campfire and rolled a log near the flames so they would have a comfy place to sit.

With the cup from a thermos, Patrick ladled soup into paper bowls that would later be burned in the fire. He'd explained that the aluminum spoons they used were light in a pack and good for the environment.

Libby ate hungrily. It was amazing how many calories one consumed by walking in the mountains. Neither she nor Patrick spoke. What was there to say? He didn't really want her here. Not to replace Charlise. And beyond that, they were nothing to each other. Virtual strangers. Except she normally didn't go around kissing strangers. She jumped when an owl hooted nearby. Though she was wearing a long-sleeved shirt and the day had been warm, she scrambled to find her jacket. Huddling into the welcome warmth, she stared into the fire and tried not to think about the night to come.

If she had any hope of convincing Patrick that she was capable of filling Charlise's shoes, she had to act as if spending a night in the dark, scary woods was no big deal.

She stared into the mesmerizing red and gold flames, listening to the pop and crackle of the burning wood. The scent of wood smoke was pleasant…a connection, perhaps, to her ancestors who had lived closer to the land.

She and Patrick had eaten their meal in complete silence. Libby was okay with that. All she wanted to do now was get through this overnight endurance test without embarrassing herself.

She cleared her throat. "So, it's already dark. And it's awfully early to go to bed. What do people do in the woods when they camp out during the winter?"

Patrick's face was all planes and angles in the glow of the fire. He was a chameleon—dashing and elegant as a Kavanagh millionaire, but now, a ruggedly masculine man with unlimited physical power and capability. Looking at him gave her a funny feeling in the pit of her stomach.

The sensation was no secret. She was seriously in lust with her reluctant boss, despite his arrogance and his refusal to take her seriously. He could be funny and charming. He had been remarkably patient, even when saddled with his mother's charity case.

But the truth was, he didn't want her on his team. And when it came to the attraction that simmered between them? Well, that was never going to amount to anything, no matter how many hours they spent alone in the woods. She pressed her knees together, her heart beating a ragged tempo as she waited for an answer to what was one part rhetorical question and the other part a need to break the intimate quiet.

If she had a tad more experience, or if she honestly believed that Patrick felt a fraction of the sexual tension that was making her jumpy, she might make a move on him. But despite his kiss—which was really more of a hands-on apology—she didn't delude herself that he had any real interest in her.

Women like Charlise were more his type. Athletic superwomen. Not timid females afraid of the shadows.

Besides, she had to stay focused on starting her life over. She was on her own. She had to be strong.

She had almost forgotten her question when he finally answered.

# Five

"Speaking for myself, I suppose it depends on who I'm with."

Patrick wasn't immune to the intimacy of the moment. He still reeled from the impact of the kiss. But all else aside, his mother would kill him if he played around with Libby. Libby was emotionally fragile and just coming out of a very rough period in her life. He couldn't take advantage of her vulnerability, even if she was already worming her way into his heart.

A part of him wanted to tell her how much fun sleeping-bag sex could be. But that would be crossing the line, and Libby Parkhurst was off-limits. He'd be exaggerating anyway. Most of the women he'd been serious about would run for the hills if he suggested anything of the sort.

It occurred to him suddenly that his love of outdoor adventure had largely been segregated from his romantic life. He hiked with his brothers. He took clients out in the woods with Charlise. But he'd never really wanted to bring a woman along in a personal, *intimate* sense.

Yet with Libby, he was tempted. Unfortunately, temptation was as far as it went. He had to keep her at a distance or this whole scenario might blow up in his face. Particularly when he had to fire her.

He picked up a tiny twig and tossed it into the fire. "You can always listen to music. Did you bring an iPod? It was on the list."

Libby nodded, her profile disarmingly feminine in the firelight. "I did. But if I have earbuds in, I won't be able to hear the wild animals when they come to rip me limb from limb."

Patrick chuckled. Despite Libby's lack of qualifications for the job as his assistant, he enjoyed her wry take on life. He also respected the fact that she acknowledged her fears without being crippled by them. As if he needed more reasons to be intrigued by her. But that didn't make her an outdoorswoman.

"I won't let anything happen to you, I swear." It was true. Libby might not be the one to cover the maternity leave, but he felt an overwhelming urge to protect her.

Eventually, Libby needed a moment of privacy in the woods. He had known it was coming. But he was pretty sure she wasn't comfortable about the dark.

When she stood up, she hedged. "I, uh…"

"You need to go to the bathroom before we call it a night."

"Yes."

He'd seen her blush before. Right now her face was probably poppy red. But he couldn't tell in the gloom. He handed her a flashlight. "Do you want me to go with you, or shall I stay here and face the fire?"

Long silence.

"Face the fire. But if I'm not back in ten minutes, send out the rescue squad."

Again, that easy humor. He sat and concentrated on the flames, feeling the heat on his face. His libido thrummed on high alert. It had never occurred to him that spending a night in the woods with Libby Parkhurst would test his self-control.

He had forgotten to glance at his watch when she left. How long had she been gone? Now she had *him* hearing all sorts of menacing sounds in the forest. "Libby," he called out. "You okay?"

He held his breath until she answered.

"I'm fine." Her voice echoed from a distance, so he stayed put.

At last she reappeared. "What time do we need to be up in the morning?" she asked.

"I'll get breakfast going…most importantly, a pot of coffee. You can pop out of your tent whenever you're ready."

"What about our packs?"

"I'll take care of it. When you get in your tent, make sure to take your boots off and put them by the exit. That way you won't get your sleeping bag muddy. The bedding I brought is warmer than the type we use in April. I hope you'll be comfortable."

"I'll be fine. Good night, Patrick."

He wished he could say the same. He was wired and horny. That was a dangerous combination.

With moves he had practiced a million times, he scattered the coals and made sure the fire was not in danger of spreading while they slept. Then he took both packs and hung them from a nearby treetop.

After crawling into his own tent and taking off his boots, he zipped the nylon flap and got settled for the night. His sleeping bag was high-tech and very comfortable. The temperature outside was perfect for snuggling into his down cocoon and sleeping.

Which didn't explain why he lay on his back and stared into the dark. The noises of the night were familiar to him. Hooting owls. Sighing wind. The *click-clack* of bare winter branches rubbing together.

Libby's tent was no more than four or five feet away from his. If he concentrated, he thought he might be able to hear her breathing.

He was almost asleep, when a female whisper roused him.

"Patrick. Are you awake?"

"I am now." He pretended to be gruff.

"What am I supposed to do if a bear tries to eat my tent?"

He grinned, even though she couldn't see. "Libby. People camp out in this part of the country all the time. We're not far from the Smoky Mountains. It's perfectly safe, I swear."

"I was kidding. Mostly. And I'm not being a wimp. I just want to be prepared for anything. But people *do* get attacked by bears. I went online and did a search."

"Are you sure you weren't reading stories about grizzlies? We don't have those in North Carolina."

"No. It was black bears. A woman died. They found her camera and she had been taking pictures."

"I remember the story you're talking about. But that was a long time ago and the woman, unfortunately, got too close to the bear."

"But what if the bear gets too close to me?"

He laughed. "Would you like to come sleep in my tent?" As soon as the words left his mouth, he regretted them. He hadn't consciously meant to flirt with her, but the feelings were there.

Long silence. "You mean with you?"

"Well, it doesn't make much sense just to swap places. If it will help you be more comfortable, I'm sure we can manage to squeeze you in here if we try."

Another, longer silence. "No, thank you. I'm fine. Really."

"Your choice." He paused. "Tell me, Libby. Did your family never vacation outdoors? National parks? Boating adventures? Anything like that?"

He heard the sound of rustling nylon as she squirmed to get comfortable.

"No. But I have a working knowledge of all the major museums in Europe, and I can order a meal at a Michelin-starred restaurant in three languages. I've summered in the Swiss Alps and wintered in Saint Lucia. Still, I've never cooked a hot dog over a campfire."

"Poor little rich girl."

"Not funny, Patrick. I happen to know the Kavanaghs are loaded. So you can't make fun of me."

"*Can't* or shouldn't?"

She laughed, the warm sound sneaking down inside him and making him feel something both arousing and uncomfortable.

"I'm going to sleep now," she said.

"See you in the morning."

Aeons later, Libby groaned. Morning light meant the dawn of a new day, but she was too warm and comfortable to care. For the past hour, she had actually been sleeping peacefully. Now, however, she had to go to the bathroom. And unlike any normal morning, she couldn't crawl back into bed afterward, because she would be completely awake.

She felt as if she had barely slept all night. Every noise was magnified in her imagination. She would doze off finally, and then minutes later some ominous sound would wake her up. It was an endless cycle.

To make matters worse, Patrick had fallen asleep almost instantly after their "bear" conversation. She knew this, because he'd snored. Not an obnoxious, chain-saw sound, but a quiet masculine rumble.

How did he do it? How did he sleep like a baby in the middle of the woods? Her hips were sore from lying on the ground, even with the pad, and she didn't know how *anyone* could manage restful slumber without some white noise.

Hiking enthusiasts talked about the peace and quiet of nature. Clearly they had never actually spent a night in the outdoors. The forest was *not* a silent place.

Though the temperatures were supposed to hit the sixties again this afternoon as the February warm spell lingered, this morning, there was a definite nip in the air. She shivered as she sat up and fumbled her way into her jacket. She could already smell the coffee Patrick had promised.

She rummaged in her pocket for the small cosmetic case she'd brought with her. A comb and a mirror and some unscented lip balm. That was it. Fortunately, the mirror was tiny, because she didn't really want to see her reflection. She had a feeling that her appearance fell somewhere between "dragged through a bush backward" and "one step away from zombie."

Putting on boots was her first challenge. Then, after struggling to tame her hair and redo her ponytail, she shook her head in defeat. She didn't need to impress Patrick with her looks. Why did it matter?

When she unzipped her tent and climbed out, she didn't glance in Patrick's direction. Instead, she headed off into the relative privacy of the forest. After taking care of her most urgent need, she returned to the campsite. Patrick looked rested, but his hair was rumpled and his jaw was shadowed with dark stubble.

Still, he looked gorgeous and sexy. Life wasn't fair at all.

He looked up from his contemplation of the fire when she sat down. "Mornin'," he said. The word was gruff.

She nodded, unable to come up with a scintillating response. The mood between them was undeniably awkward.

He poured her a cup of coffee. "Careful, it's hot."

"Thanks." Adding sugar and a packet of artificial creamer, she inhaled the steam, hoping the diffused caffeine would jump-start her sluggish brain. So far, the five-word conversation between her and her boss was taxing her will to live.

Two cups later, she began to feel slightly human. Even so, the fact that she had been wearing the same clothes for twenty-four hours made her long for a hot shower.

"What next?" she asked. The sooner Patrick taught her the drill, the sooner they could go home.

"We break down camp. With a group event, we'll have the camp stoves set up right over there. The guys that packed in the food and supplies will be your assistants. The meal is simple, homemade oatmeal with cinnamon and brown sugar for those who want it. Precooked bacon that we crisp up in a skillet. Whole oranges. And of course, coffee."

"Will I have to cook the oatmeal?"

"No. Only warm it. It's mostly a matter of being organized and making sure everyone gets served quickly. They're always eager to get started on the rest of the day, so we try not to drag out the meal process."

"I can handle that."

"You ready to head out?"

*Gulp.* Of course. She noticed he didn't say "head home." Clearly there was more to be learned.

She paid close attention as Patrick showed her how to

break down the tents and put out the fire. Once they re-loaded their packs, the site was pristine. It went without saying that a company like Silver Reflections would re-spect the sanctity of the natural world.

Patrick wasn't very talkative this morning. Perhaps he was regretting their momentary lapse. Or maybe he had other issues on his mind. Losing Charlise's expertise for six months had to be frustrating for him. Maybe everyone would have been a lot happier if Patrick had simply stood up to Maeve and told her he would find his own, far more qualified, temporary employee.

Still, even given the circumstances far beyond her com-fort zone, Libby realized she really wanted this job. Be-neath the physical challenges she was experiencing lurked exhilaration that she was facing her fears and conquering them…or at least trying to…

This morning's hike was shorter, no more than three or four miles. And Patrick's pace was more of a stroll than a death march. With the sun shining and the birds singing, it was almost easy to dismiss her sleepless night.

When they stopped for a snack, Patrick didn't take the time to unpack any kind of seating tarp. Instead, they leaned against trees. Recent rains had left the ground damp, particularly beneath the top layer of rotting leaves. He fished salted peanuts and beef jerky from his pocket. "This will give you energy," he said.

"Do I look that bad?"

His lips quirked. "Maybe a little frayed around the edges. Nothing to worry about. But it will be several hours before we get home, so you have to keep up your strength."

She bit off a piece of jerky, grimacing at the taste. "That sounds ominous. What's next? Building a canoe from a tree? Making blow darts from poison berries? Killing and skinning a wild animal with my bare hands?"

Patrick chuckled. "You've been watching too many movies."

"Then what?"

"We're going underground."

Her stomach fell somewhere in the vicinity of her boots. "Um, no. I don't think so. I got locked in a closet for several hours when I was a little kid and I've been claustrophobic ever since. I don't do caves."

It seemed as if he were baiting her, but she couldn't be sure.

"No caves in these mountains," he said. "It's the wrong kind of geology. You might find some large rock overhangs that provide shelter…but not the places where spelunkers investigate tunnels deep into the earth."

"Then what?"

"A mine." He didn't smile. In fact, his face was carefully expressionless.

Was this the part where she was supposed to throw up her hands and say "I quit"? "What kind of mine?" she asked, thinking about every Appalachian horror story she had heard about shafts collapsing and miners being buried alive.

"Years ago, it was one of hundreds of silver mines in the area, but it's long since been tapped out."

"Then why go in?"

"The claustrophobia you mentioned is a very real fear for many people. When we bring groups out, I go down into the mine with three at a time. Usually, the participants have been prepped in advance about what to discuss. Something simple, but work-related. We sit in the dark as they try to carry on a conversation without panicking."

"And if someone *does* freak out?"

"Their colleagues talk them through it…part of the team-building aspect. You'd be surprised. Sometimes it's the tough macho guys who can't handle it. It's an eye-opener all the way around."

"Well, thanks for telling me about it," she said, her voice high-pitched and squeaky. "I'll do absolutely everything you want me to do *above*ground, no questions asked. But I think I'll take a pass on the mine thing. I hope that's not a deal breaker."

Patrick took her hands, staring into her eyes like a hypnotist. "You can trust me, Libby, I swear."

She exhaled, an audibly jerky sigh. "This might be a good time to mention that my childhood was spent learning how to be scared of everything. My mom wouldn't take me into Central Park because of muggers. No Macy's Thanksgiving Parade because of lurking kidnappers in the crowd. If a spider ever had the temerity to invade our apartment, things went to DEFCON 1 in a hurry. She didn't want me to have a boyfriend, so she told me I could get pregnant from kissing."

"You and I are in trouble, then."

She ignored his attempt at levity. "I was afraid of drowning in the bathtub and being exposed to radioactivity from the microwave. My Halloween candy had to be checked for razor blades, even though it was all a gift from our neighbors across the hall, people we had known for years. I could go on, but you get the idea."

"You know that your mother had serious issues."

"Yes." It was hard to admit it out loud.

"People don't commit suicide for no reason. Your father's fall from grace may have devastated her, but surely it was more than that."

"I know." She swallowed hard, chagrined to feel hot tears threaten her composure. "I also learned to be afraid that I might be like her."

"Bullshit."

Patrick's forceful curse shocked her.

He squeezed her hands, and released her only to pull her against his chest for a brief hug. Then he stepped back and brushed a damp strand of hair from her forehead. The compassion in his gray-blue eyes stripped her raw.

"Libby," he said quietly, "you may not be the right person for this job, but you're strong and independent and amazingly resilient. Not once have you whined about what the last year has been like for you. During terrible, tragic circumstances, you cared for your mother when she couldn't care for herself. You did everything a loving daughter could do. And even though it may seem like it wasn't enough, that's not true."

"I tried to get help for her."

"By selling all your clothes and jewelry to pay for treatment."

"How did you know that?"

He shrugged. "Charlise told me."

Of course. "It wasn't like I had a use for all that stuff," she said.

"Doesn't matter. You gave everything you had. You walked a hard road. You're nothing like her, I promise. Nothing at all. And you don't have to go down into a mine to prove it."

# Six

---

Patrick felt out of his depth. He was neither a grief counselor nor a psychiatrist. All he could do was make sure Libby knew how much he respected and admired her. And better yet, he could resist the urge to muddy the waters with sex.

She stared at him, her expression impossible to decipher. "I've changed my mind," she said quietly. "I want to do it. Not to impress you or to convince you to let me keep the job, but to prove something to myself."

"There are other ways," he said quietly, now suddenly positive that he had made a mistake in bringing her.

"But we're here. And the time is right. Let's go."

She took off down the clearly marked trail, forcing him to follow along behind. Their destination was a little over two miles away. With Libby setting the pace, they made it to the mine's entrance in forty-five minutes. She stopped dead when he called out to her.

The mine was unmarked for obvious reasons. No reason to tempt kids and reckless adults into doing something stupid.

He caught Libby's arm. "We've had engineers reinforce the first quarter mile. Enough to withstand even a mild earthquake. We do get those around here. I wouldn't take clients in there if it was dangerous."

"I know." She bit her lip. "How do we do this?"

"We'll carry our packs in our arms. I'll go first, using a headlamp. You stay on my heels. When we get to a certain spot, I'll spread something on the ground and we'll sit. At any moment if you change your mind, all you have to do is say so."

"How long do you normally stay underground?"

"An hour."

When she paled, he backpedaled quickly. "But we can always walk in and simply turn around and walk out." He hesitated. Was his role to encourage her or to talk her out of this? "Are you sure, Libby?"

She nodded, her pupils dilated. "I'm sure. But since I'm pretty nervous, you won't mind if I disappear into the woods for a minute?"

He looked at her blankly.

"To relieve myself."

"Ah." While she was gone, he followed suit and then waited for her return.

Though the day was bright and sunny, Libby's skin was clammy when she reappeared. He touched her shoulder. "You might want to roll down your sleeves and put on your jacket. It will be cool in the mine." They had shed layers as they walked and the air grew warmer.

Libby did as he suggested and then stared at him. "What now?"

"Let's do this." He pushed aside the undergrowth that had taken over the mine's entrance since last year. Facing him was a wooden door set into the dirt. He wrestled it loose and pushed it aside. "Door stays open," he said. "No getting locked inside, I swear."

"Is that supposed to make me feel better?"

He shot her a glance over his shoulder. She was smiling, but in her eyes he saw apprehension. Even so, her jaw was set, her resolve visible.

"Follow me," he said.

Libby put one foot in front of the other, blindly trusting Patrick Kavanagh to lead her into the bowels of the earth. Months ago when she and her mother were grief stricken and displaced, trying to start a new life, Libby had been anxious and stressed and worried.

But not like this. Her skin crawled with unease. People were meant to exist in the light. Her heartbeat deafened her. "Patrick!" She called out to him, her stomach churning.

He stopped immediately, dropping his pack and turning to face her. The beam of his headlamp blinded her. They weren't far into the mine. Daylight still filtered in behind them.

"Steady," he said. Knowing his eyes were on her only amplified her embarrassment.

She held up a hand. "Don't touch me. I'm fine."

Patrick nodded slowly. "Okay."

Suddenly, she wanted to throw herself into his arms. He was strong and self-assured and utterly calm. She was a mess. No wonder he thought she couldn't handle Charlise's job.

Slowly, they advanced into the mine. A quarter of a mile sounded like nothing at all. But in reality, it felt like a marathon.

Her panic mounted. No matter how slowly she breathed and how much she told herself she could do this, her chest tightened and her stomach curled. "Wait," she said. Frustration ate at her resolve. Mind over matter wasn't working.

She dropped her pack and wrapped her arms around her waist. "Give me a couple of minutes. I can make it."

Patrick dumped his pack as well and removed his head-lamp so that the light pointed at their feet. "It speaks volumes that you even tried this, Libby."

Wiping her nose with her sleeve, she shook her head. "I hate being so stupid." Now would be a good time for him to hold her and distract her with his incredibly hot and sexy body. But apparently, that wasn't going to happen anytime soon. Or ever.

"You're not stupid. Lots of people have fears…heights, spiders, clowns."

His droll comment made her laugh. "Clowns? Seriously?"

"Coulrophobia. It's a real thing."

"You're making that up."

She heard him chuckle.

"I wouldn't lie to you."

"What are you afraid of, Patrick?"

Before he could answer, a muted rumble sounded in the distance.

"Hang on, Libby," he said.

Before she could ask what or why, a roaring crash reverberated in the tunnel. Debris rained down on them, first in a gentle fall, and then in a heavy shower that choked them and pelted their heads.

She heard Patrick curse. And then she stumbled.

Patrick fumbled in total darkness for Libby's arm. They had both gone down in the chaos. His brain looked for answers even as he searched frantically for his companion. He latched onto her shoulders and shook her. "Say something, damn it. Are you hurt?"

Dragging her into his lap he ran his hands over her head and limbs, checking for injuries. When he found none, he sighed in relief. He chafed her hands and rubbed her face until she stirred.

"Patrick?" she muttered.

"I'm here." Just then, her entire body went rigid and she cried out.

"We're okay," he said firmly. "There's no need to panic."

She was silent, telling him louder than words she thought he was crazy. After a moment she tried to sit up. "What happened?"

He kept an arm around her, feeling the shudders that racked her body. Though he would walk through hot coals before admitting it, the infinite, crushing darkness was pretty damn terrifying. "I'm not exactly sure, but I can make a guess. The mine hasn't caved in. I told you we've had it checked and reinforced."

"Then what?" Her head was tucked against his shoulder, her hands curled against his chest, her fingernails digging into his shirt, as if she wanted to climb inside his skin.

"I think it was a quick tremor…a small earthquake."

"In North Carolina?"

"I told you. It happens. And we've had so damn much rain in the last three weeks, it's possible there was a landslide that blocked the entrance."

Nothing he could say was going to make the facts any more palatable. Libby's skin, at least the exposed part, was icy cold, far colder than warranted by the temperature in the mine. He worried she might be going into shock. So they had to take action…anything to break the cycle of panic and disbelief.

"I need to walk back to the entrance and see what it looks like."

Her grip on his shirtfront tightened. "Not without me."

He smiled in the dark. "Okay. But first we have to find the headlamp."

He let go of his precious cargo with one hand and sifted through the debris.

Libby was pressed so close to his chest he could feel the runaway beat of her heart. "Is it there?"

He found the elastic strap and lifted it out of the pile of dust and twigs and small stones. But when he flicked the switch, nothing happened. Feeling carefully around the outer portion of the LED lamp, he realized that the whole lens had shattered.

"It's here," he muttered. "But it's broken."

"What about our phones?"

How exactly was he supposed to answer that? Did he need to tell her they could be stranded for days and needed to preserve the batteries? On the other hand, if they were going to be rescued, it made sense to get as close to the entrance of the mine as possible. Unless, of course, there was another landslide. Highly unlikely, but possible.

"I have a couple of backup flashlights," he said. "All I have to do is locate my pack and get them. Will you be okay for a minute if I let go of you?"

"Of course."

The right words, wrong tone. She was perilously close to the breaking point.

Cursing himself for bringing her down into this hellhole, he set her aside and reached out his hands like a blind man. The first pack he found was Libby's. Since he had loaded it himself, he knew the exact contents. But he had put the flashlights in his pack, because they were heavy.

Moments later, he found his own equipment. When he located the item he wanted and flicked the switch, the small beam of light was as welcome as fresh water in the desert.

Libby stared at him owlishly. "Thank God," she said simply.

"You have stuff in your hair," he said. "Not insects," he

added quickly. Leaning forward, he combed his fingers through the ends of her ponytail and picked tiny debris from the rest of her head. "There," he said. "All better."

His conversation was nonsensical. He freely admitted that. But what in the hell were you supposed to say to the beautiful woman you were buried alive with—the very one you were hoping to keep at arms' length because she was vulnerable and trusting and not the woman you needed in your life either personally or professionally?

"It's not my real color," Libby said.

"Excuse me?" He was befuddled, maybe a little bit in shock himself.

"The color," she said. "I'm a redhead. Maybe you remember from when I was a kid. But after the mess with my father, I started dying my hair so I would blend into the crowd. Now I'm afraid to change it back."

"Tomorrow," he said firmly. "Tomorrow you should make an appointment with a stylist and go back to being you."

At last, she smiled. A weak smile, but a smile. "You are so full of it."

"I'm serious. Men love redheads."

"You know what I mean. I'm not an idiot. The chances of us getting out of here anytime soon are pretty slim. No one is expecting us back until dinnertime. That's several hours from now. And by the time they start to wonder where we are, it will be dark."

"So we'll wait," he said. "We have a decent amount of food and water. If we're careful, it will last."

"How long?" The question was stark.

"Long enough."

He got to his feet, ignoring the lash of pain in his left calf. "Come on, woman. Let's see what happened. We'll take our gear with us."

They hadn't really come all that far. It didn't take long

to retrace their steps. Unfortunately, his guess was spot-on. With or without a tremor as the inciting incident, a goodly portion of the hillside had come sliding down on top of the mine opening. Wet, sludgy earth filled the entrance. Trying to burrow out would only make the whole pile shift and slither, much like digging a hole at the beach.

But Libby looked at him with such naked hope he had to do something. "Stand back," he said. "Maybe it's not as bad as it looks."

"May I hold a flashlight, too?"

It wasn't a good idea. Batteries were like gold in their situation. Still, she needed the reassurance of sight. Later on they could sit in darkness.

He reached into his pocket for the spare flashlight and handed it to her. "I'm serious," he said. "Don't get too close."

For a moment, he was stymied. Using his bare hands to dig seemed ineffective at best, but even mentally cataloging the contents of his backpack, he couldn't think of a damn thing that might serve as a shovel.

In the end, he tucked the flashlight under his armpit and awkwardly began to gouge his fingers into the wet mess. Dry dirt wouldn't have been so bad, but the mud was a frustrating opponent.

After ten minutes of concerted effort, he had made no headway at all. Not only that, he was starting to feel dizzy. He stumbled backward, his filthy arms outstretched. "This isn't going to work. I'm sorry, Libby."

"You're hurt," she said, alarm in her voice. "You're bleeding below the knee."

He blinked, trying to focus his thoughts. Maybe adrenaline had masked his injury, because now his leg hurt like hell. "I don't want to touch the flashlight with all this gunk on my hands. Can you look at my leg?"

Libby squatted and touched his shin. "Whatever it was cut all the way through the cloth."

"Probably a piece of glass. We've found all kinds of broken bottles and crockery down here over the years."

He flinched when she carefully rolled up the leg of his pants.

"Oh, God, Patrick," she gasped. "You need stitches. Sit down so I can look at it."

"Wait. Find the tarp in my pack. We're going to have to make a place to get comfortable." *Comfortable* wasn't even on the map of where they were located. But they would take what they could get.

Libby moved quickly, locating the large tarp and spreading it with one side tucked up against the wall of the mine so they could lean against something. When she was done, he pointed to an outside zip pocket of his pack. "There's a small, thin towel in there. Can you wet it, just barely, so I can get the worst of this off?"

Libby did as he asked, but instead of giving him the towel, she took his hands in hers and began wiping his fingers clean. It was a difficult chore, especially given the lack of water.

He still held the flashlight under his arm. Though he couldn't see Libby's face, there was enough illumination for him to watch as she removed the muck. It was an intimate act…and an unselfish one…because the process dirtied her skin, as well.

But finally he was more or less back to normal.

"Sit down now," she urged.

He was happy to comply.

With his back against the wall of the mine, he took a deep breath. He felt like hell, and his leg had begun to throb viciously. There's a first aid kit," he said gruffly. "Big outer pocket. Antiseptic wipes."

Libby put a hand on his thigh, perhaps to get his attention. "You've lost a lot of blood, Patrick. A lot. The cut is four inches long and gaping."

"Clean it the best you can. We'll use butterfly bandages." The words were an effort. "I'll hold the flashlight."

It occurred to him that he could reach his own leg…do his own medical care. But he couldn't seem to work up the energy to try.

Libby's touch was deft but gentle. Wisely, she didn't waste time getting rid of all the blood. He watched her concentrate on the cut, making sure the edges were clean, dabbing at tiny bits of dirt that might cause infection later. When she was satisfied, she sat back on her heels. "I'll let it dry a minute," she said, "before I use the butterfly thingies."

"Can you get me a couple of painkillers?" he asked, hurting too much to act macho at this particular moment.

"Of course."

He took them with a sip of water and sighed. "Is the skin dry?"

Libby traced around the wound with a fingertip. "Yes." She tore open a small packet and gently affixed the Band-Aid, pulling the open edges of the cut together. It took two more before she was satisfied. "The bleeding has stopped."

"Good." He closed his eyes. "Sit between my legs," he said. "It will keep us both warm."

He needed the human contact, but more than that, he needed a connection to Libby specifically. She might be completely wrong for him on far too many levels, but right now, they had each other and no one else. He wanted to feel her and know she was okay.

# Seven

Libby felt like she was in a dream. But when she settled between Patrick's thighs, her legs outstretched, her back against his chest, the situation got a whole lot more real.

Strong arms wrapped around her waist. Big masculine hands clasped beneath her breasts. Patrick's breath warmed the side of her neck. "Are you going to be okay?" she asked. The tenor of his breathing alarmed her. That and his silence.

"It's just a cut. Don't worry about it."

She might be inexperienced when it came to medical care, but she wasn't stupid. Patrick needed a proper hospital, an IV of fluids and red meat. Instead, he was stuck down here with her.

"What time is it?" she asked, feeling her anxiety rise again now that the immediate crisis was past.

"We have to turn off the flashlights," he said quietly, the words ruffling her hair.

She didn't know which part worried her the most—the

fact that he deliberately ignored her question, or the regression to pitch-black darkness. Without vision, the world seemed ominous.

"Do you sing?" she asked.

He groaned. "You don't want to hear that, I promise."

"I'm sorry, Patrick, but if you don't talk to me, I might go bonkers."

"Okay, okay." The words held amusement.

"Tell me about your family. My mother used to keep in touch with Maeve all the time, but I don't really know much about the Kavanagh clan. What are your brothers up to these days?"

"Liam is the oldest. He married a woman named Zoe who is sort of a free spirit. We love her, and she's a perfect match for my stick-in-the-mud brother."

"Go on."

"You saw Dylan at the pub. His wife is Mia. Dylan adopted her little girl."

"Next is Aidan?"

"That's right. He and Emma divide their time between New York and Silver Glen. Then comes Gavin. He runs a cybersecurity firm here in Silver Glen. His wife is Cassidy, and they have twin baby girls."

"What about Conor? Wasn't he the big skier in the family?"

"Still is. He ended up marrying a girl he knew way back in high school. Her name is Ellie."

"Which leaves you and James…is that his name?"

"Yep. My baby brother…who happens to be four inches taller than I am and thirty pounds heavier. We call him the gentle giant."

"You love him. I hear it in your voice."

"Well, when you're the last two in a string of seven, you end up bonding. It was either that or be terrorized by our siblings on a regular basis. With James on my side, I had a tactical advantage."

"Your mother takes credit for marrying off the first five. I suppose you and James are next in her sights."

"Not gonna happen."

The blunt, flat-toned response shocked her. "Oh?"

"Let me rephrase that. I can't speak for my brother, but I'm not interested in tying the knot. Earlier, you asked me what I was afraid of and I never got a chance to answer you. The truth is, it's marriage. I tried it once and it didn't pan out. So I plan on being happily single."

She turned toward him, which was dumb, because she couldn't see his face. "You're divorced?"

"Worse than that."

"She died?" Libby gaped in the darkness, horrified, feeling as if she had stepped in the middle of a painful past Patrick didn't want to share. But now that the door was open, she couldn't ignore the peek inside this complicated man.

Patrick sighed, his chest rising and falling. He pulled her back against him. "No. The marriage was annulled."

It was a good thing Patrick was willing to talk about his past, because the only thing keeping Libby from climbing the walls was concentrating on the sound of his voice. All around her, the dark encroached. Would they have to sleep here and wake up here and slowly starve to death?

Panic fluttered in her chest. "What happened?" she asked.

Patrick wasn't a fan of rehashing his youthful mistakes, but he and Libby had to do something to maintain a sense of normalcy. The medicine had dulled the pain in his leg, though he still felt alarmingly weak.

He rested his chin on her head, inhaling the faint scent of her skin. Her upper-class upbringing meant she'd been taught the rules of polite behavior at an early age. He was sure Libby would never ask that kind of personal question under different circumstances.

But here in the mine, such considerations were less important than the need to feel connected.

He played with the fingers of her right hand, fingers that were bare. Where were the diamonds, the pearls, the precious gems this young, wealthy woman had worn? All sold for her mother's treatment. Libby's mom had betrayed that sacrifice by killing herself.

The picture of Libby he'd had in the beginning was fading rapidly, the colors blurred by the reality of who she was. She'd been a Madison Avenue heiress...no doubt about that. But Libby Parkhurst was so much more than the sum of what she had lost.

His feelings toward her were confusing. He wanted to protect her, both physically and emotionally. And though it was disconcerting as hell, he was beginning to *want* her. In the way a man wants a woman.

Even here in this dank, dark mine shaft—and even though he had a throbbing wound in his leg—his body reacted to the feel of her in his arms. Their relationship had been thrown into fast-forward. He was bombarded with emotions—tenderness, affection and definitely admiration. For a woman who had barely been able to contemplate walking into the mine shaft and back out again, it was nothing short of remarkable that she was still able to function, considering what had happened.

He realized she was still waiting for an answer about his marriage. "My girlfriend got pregnant," he said. "One of those terrible clichés that turns out to be true. I'd been careful to protect both of us, but..."

"Accidents happen."

"Yes. My brothers and I had been brought up with a very strict code of honor. Her parents wanted us to get married, so I agreed. In hindsight, I doubt my mother was thrilled, but what could she do?"

"And the annulment?"

"When the little boy was born, he was dark-skinned... African-American. Even for a girl who was terrified to tell her parents she was involved in a mixed-race relationship and even though she was embarrassed to admit she'd been cheating on her boyfriend, it was clear that the gig was up. We didn't need to have a paternity test done. The truth stared us in the face."

"Oh, Patrick. You must have been devastated."

He winced, even now reacting to a painful, fleeting memory of what that day had done to him. "We'd been living together as husband and wife. We had both graduated from high school...rented a small house. Even though I'd been upset and angry and not at all ready to become a father, after nine months, I'd finally come around to the idea. I was so excited about that little boy."

"And then you lost him."

"Yes. I walked out of the hospital and never looked back. I went home. Slept in the bed where I'd grown up. But nothing was the same. You can't rewrite history and undo your mistakes. All you can do is move forward and not make those same mistakes again."

He wanted to know what Libby was thinking, but he kept on talking. It was cathartic to rehash what had been a chaotic, deeply painful time in his life. It was a subject never broached by the Kavanagh clan. They had swept it under the rug and moved on.

"I didn't abandon the baby," he said, remembering the infant's tiny face. "I want you to know that. His father stepped up. As soon as the annulment was final, he married the mother of his child and they made a family."

"You must have been so hurt."

It was true. He'd been crushed. But he had never let on how much it affected him.

"Adolescence is tough for everybody," he muttered.

Libby turned on her side, nestling her cheek against his chest and drawing up her knees until they threatened his manhood. "You're a good man, Patrick Kavanagh."

He stroked her hair. "I'm sorry about this," he said.

Libby sighed audibly. "It will be something to tell our children one day." She stopped dead, realizing what she had said.

"Don't worry about it, Libby. I'm a very popular uncle, and I like it that way."

"Have you told Maeve how you feel?"

"I think she guesses. She hasn't quite put the marital screws on me like she has the others."

"I'm warning you, it's only a matter of time. You'd better watch your step around her. She's wonderful, but sneaky."

After that, they dozed. Patrick dreamed restlessly, always fighting an ominous foe. Each time he awoke, his arms tightened around Libby. She was his charge, his responsibility. He would do everything in his power to make sure she got out of this mess in one piece.

At last, they couldn't ignore the rumbles of hungry stomachs. "What do you want?" he asked. "Beef jerky or peanuts?"

"I'll take the nuts, I guess."

He handed her the water. "Three sips, no more. We have to be smart about rationing."

"Can we please turn on one of the phones and find out what time it is? Do you think there's any hope of getting a signal down here? We're near the surface."

"I'll look. And no. I don't think there's a chance at all of having a signal."

"You really suck at this cheering up thing."

He checked the time, oddly comforted by the familiar glow of the phone screen. "Seven fifteen."

"So it's dark outside."

"Yes." He turned off the electronic device and stowed it. "It doesn't really matter, though, does it? Not to us?"

"I suppose not." She sighed. "Tell me something else. Do you have big plans for the weekend?"

"I'm flying up to New York Friday morning to do an orientation for one of the teams coming in April. Peabody Rushford is a world-renowned accounting firm with A-list clients. We'll sit around a big conference table, and I'll go over the checklist with all of them. They'll ask questions…"

"May I go with you?"

He paused, taken aback. Maybe Libby was simply trying to convince herself she wouldn't still be trapped underground come Friday. "I'm not sure there's any reason for you to be there," he said. "I don't want to hurt your feelings, but this job is not the one for you. I think you know that."

"Maybe so. But I was thinking of a more personal agenda."

His mind raced, already inventing sexual scenarios where he and Libby ended up naked on soft sheets. "What kind of agenda?"

"I haven't been back to my building since the day my mother and I had to leave. I thought I could go see it. I can't get inside the apartment, of course. Someone else lives there now. But I think even standing on the street would give me some closure."

"Then of course you can come with me," he said. "I wish I could fly us up there in my new toy. I bought a used Cessna recently, but it's still being overhauled. So we'll have to take the jet."

"*Now* who sounds like the poor little rich kid?" she teased.

"You've got me. But to be fair, the Kavanaghs share the jet with several others owners."

"Well, that makes it okay, of course."

"If I were you, I don't think I would alienate the only human being standing between me and solitary confinement."

"Not funny, Patrick."

"Sorry."

They sat in silence. The teasing had kept the darkness at bay for a few moments, but the truth returned. They were trapped...with no hope of rescue until morning at least, and maybe not even then.

Libby stood up, accidentally elbowing him in the ribs. "I have to stretch," she said.

"Don't go far."

"Hilarious, Kavanagh."

He might as well stand up, too. But when he moved, he cursed as pain shot up his leg, hot and vicious.

Libby crouched beside him. "Give me the flashlight."

"Why? We need to save the battery."

"I'm going to look at your leg. Don't argue with me."

She was cute when she was indignant. He surrendered the flashlight wordlessly.

In a brightly lit room, he would have been able to examine his own leg. With nothing but the thin beam of the flashlight, though, he had to rely on Libby for an up-close diagnosis. "How does it look?"

"Bad."

"Bad as in 'needs an antibiotic,' or bad as in 'heading for amputation'?"

She turned the flashlight toward his face, blinding him. "That isn't funny. If we stay in here much longer, you could be in serious trouble."

He covered his eyes. "I choose to laugh instead of cry."

"I'll bet you've never cried in your life. Alpha males don't do that."

"I cried when my father disappeared."

# Eight

"Oh, Patrick." Libby's heart turned over. She would bet every dollar of her first paycheck that he hadn't meant to say something so revealing. She sat back down, feeling warm and almost secure when he enfolded her in his arms again. "I know we touched on this during my interview, and I'm sorry to open up old wounds... Did he really just go away?"

"I was a little kid, so some of my memories are fuzzy... but I've heard the story a hundred times. My father was obsessed with finding the silver mine that launched the Kavanagh fortunes generations ago. He would go out for days at a time...and then one weekend, he simply never came back."

"I'm sorry."

"It was a long time ago."

Libby had a blinding revelation, which was really pretty funny considering she was sitting in total darkness. She and Patrick had both been betrayed by their fathers. But luckily for Patrick, *his* mother was a rock.

"Did anyone have a valid theory about what happened?"

"In the beginning, there were lots of possibilities. The police posed the idea that he might have simply abandoned us, started a new life. But his passport was in the safe at home and none of his clothes or prized possessions were missing. He couldn't have left the country, and since none of the family vehicles had been taken, the final conclusion was that he had been killed somewhere in the mountains."

"You mean by wild animals?"

"It's possible. Or he could have fallen."

"But his body was never found."

"Exactly. Which meant that everyone's best educated guess was that my dad went down inside a mine—looking for remnants of a silver vein—and the mine collapsed."

"Oh."

Patrick's arms tightened around her. "This probably isn't the best conversation for us to be having at the moment."

"It does have a certain macabre theme."

"Remember, Libby…this mine we're in *didn't* collapse. It's just that the entrance has been blocked."

"A fine distinction that I'm sorry to say is not very comforting."

"You have *me*. That's something."

Actually, that was a lot. Patrick's reassuring presence was keeping most of her panic at bay…at least for stretches at a time. But their enforced intimacy had created another problem.

In the two weeks she had worked for him, she'd done her best to ignore the fact that he was a handsome, funny, intellectually stimulating man on whom she had a perfectly understandable crush. She'd kept her distance and been a model employee.

But now, with his strong arms holding her tight and his rumbly voice giving her goose bumps when his warm breath tickled her neck and cheek, she was suddenly, madly infatuated. That's all it was. An adrenaline-born rush of arousal. Part of the fight-or-flight response.

The same thing would have happened if she and Patrick had been cave people fleeing from a saber-toothed tiger. Of course later, once they were safe, they might have had wild monkey sex on a fur pelt by the roaring fire.

Her mouth went dry, and the pit of her stomach felt funny. "Patrick?" Clearly her brain cells were being starved of oxygen. Or maybe she was truly losing it, because the next words that came out of her mouth were totally inappropriate. "Will you kiss me?"

She felt his whole body stiffen. "Never mind," she said quickly. "That was just the claustrophobia talking."

"We're not going to die. I promise." His voice sounded funny…as if he had swallowed something down his windpipe.

"And by extrapolation I'm supposed to understand that imminent death is the only situation in which you could see yourself kissing me? Because I'm *one of your mother's misfits*, and a general pain in the ass?"

"You're not playing fair, Libby."

She turned in his embrace, her hands finding his face in the dark. His jaw was stubbly. She rubbed her thumbs over his strong chin. "Kiss me, Patrick," she whispered. "I know I'm taking advantage of you in your weakened state, but please. I've wondered for days what kind of woman you want. I know it's not me. Under the circumstances, though, you could bend the rules…right?"

"Libby, darlin'…"

The way he said her name was pure magic. "I'm listening."

He made a noise that sounded like choked laughter. "You were never spanked as a child, were you?"

She shrugged. "My nannies loved me. So, no. Is that an offer?"

"What about the spiders and the mud and the dungeon ambience?"

"Are you stalling?"

"I don't want you to be embarrassed when we get out of here."

"Embarrassed that I asked for a kiss, or embarrassed that I kissed my boss? I don't think that last one is a problem. You've pretty well admitted that my days are numbered when it comes to working for Silver Reflections."

His hands tangled in her hair, his lips brushing her forehead. "For the record, I haven't completely made up my mind about your status at Silver Reflections. Plus, kissing will make us want other things."

"Too late," she said, breathless...longing. "I already want those other things, but I'm willing to settle for a kiss."

"God, you're a brat."

Somehow, the way he said it turned the words into a husky compliment. "Shall I leave you alone, Patrick?"

His fingers tightened on her skull. "No. That's not what I want at all."

Before she could respond, he angled her head and found her mouth with his. The first kiss was barely perceptible... no more than a faint brush of lips to lips. Even so, she melted into him, stung by a wild burst of hunger that couldn't be satisfied by anything less than full body contact.

The kiss deepened. Patrick muttered something, but she was too lost to translate it. They had done this once before. That "sort of an apology" kiss they had shared in the woods. But she hadn't taken him seriously at the time. She'd thought he was just being nice. Charming. Offering sophisticated reparation for a thoughtless, hurtful mistake.

This was different. This was desperation. Need. Raw, unscripted masculine hunger.

Her fingers fumbled with his shirt buttons, tearing at them until she could rest her cheek against hot male skin. She nipped a flat nipple with her teeth. "I'm getting used to the dark," she whispered.

He groaned. "I'm not." He did his own version of seek-and-find, palming her breasts and squeezing them gently. "I want to see you...all of you."

There were no words to describe the feel of his hands on her bare flesh. It didn't matter that his fingers were probably still mud streaked...or that she shivered with her shirt unbuttoned. She was drowning in pleasure.

Need became a demanding beast, telling her there was a way...insisting that the less-than-perfect circumstances weren't as important as the yearning to take Patrick Kavanagh and make him hers. Her brain made a bid for common sense, reminding her that getting involved sexually with Patrick Kavanagh was a really bad idea.

But other parts of her body spoke more loudly. "How big is this tarp?" she asked, her fingers trembling as she unbuckled his belt.

Patrick found himself in uncharted territory. At any given moment he could find his way through a dense forest on a moonless night with no more than a compass and his knowledge of the mountains. Right now, however, he was a blind man struggling in quicksand.

This was insanity. Complete and utter disregard for the seriousness of their situation. He had to call a halt...

"Touch me," he begged.

When Libby's fingers closed around his erection, he sucked in a sharp breath.

"You fascinate me, Patrick," she said softly, her firm

touch on his body perfect in every way…as if they had been lovers forever and knew exactly what the other liked.

"I'm no different from any other guy," he croaked, feeling his temperature rise as sweat broke out on his brow. "We see, we want, we take."

"And what if *I* take *you*?"

His heart stopped. He tried to remember all the reasons why he was supposed to be a gentleman. The family connection. Libby's recent losses. His mother's disapproval.

Nothing worked. He wanted Libby. Badly. Enough to ignore his better judgment.

After that, it was only a matter of logistics. It could work. Not ideal, but doable. He fumbled with his pants, trying to lower them, but Libby was plastered against his chest, and he couldn't bear to shove her away, even for a moment.

"Wait," she cried. "Stop."

"Damn it, woman, this was *your* idea." He would stop if he had to, but why in the hell was she blowing hot and cold?

She put her hand over his mouth. "Listen," she said, urgency in her tone. "I heard something."

Patrick heard something, too. But it was the sound of his libido crying out in frustrated disbelief. "What are you talking about?"

"Shut up and listen."

Now she was making him mad.

And then he heard it. A scraping sound. And something else. Something human. *Holy hell.* "Button your blouse."

He struggled with his own clothing, and then cursed when he needed her help to stand up. The pain meds had worn off, and his leg was one big ache. Funny how lust was a stunningly effective narcotic. Fumbling for the flashlight, he took Libby's hand and they moved forward.

"We can't get too close," she whispered.

He squeezed her hand. "Cover your ears. I'm going to yell. *"We're down here!"* His plea echoed in their prison.

But from the other side of the mud and rock, a garbled response told him someone had heard the three simple words.

Libby's fingernails dug into his palm. "Who do you think it is?"

"Does it matter? As long as it's not the Grim Reaper, I'm a fan."

They clung to each other, barely breathing.

Suddenly, an unwelcome sensation intruded. "Libby," he said hoarsely. "My ankle is wet."

She reached inside his jacket. "Is that a flashlight in your pocket, or are you glad to see me?" Dropping to her knees, she shone the light on his leg. "Oh, hell, Patrick. The butterfly strips came loose. You're bleeding like a stuck pig. We have to sit you down. Let me find the tarp."

"No," he muttered, feeling woozy. "A little dirt won't hurt me." Leaning on Libby with a death grip, he bent his knees and stumbled onto his butt, cursing when his leg cried out in agony.

She hovered at his side, crouching and combing her fingers through his hair. "Are you okay?"

"Never better."

Without fanfare, a hole opened up in the mud. The unmistakable sounds of shoveling reverberated off the tunnel walls.

A voice, oddly disembodied, floated through the twelve-inch opening. "Patrick! You okay, man?"

Patrick swallowed. "I'm fine."

He licked his lips, shaking all over. "That's James, my brother. How did he know we were here?"

Libby put her arms around him, holding him close. "To quote a man I know, does it matter? Hang on, Patrick. It won't be much longer."

At last, the opening was large enough so they could

lean through and allow themselves to be tugged out like bears from honey pots. Patrick staggered but made it to his feet. He blinked, seeing four of his brothers staring at him. He must look worse than he thought. "Thanks for coming, guys."

And then his world went black.

Libby had her arm around Patrick's waist, but she was no match for his deadweight when he lost consciousness. They both went down hard, despite the fact that James reached for his brother.

"What's wrong with him?" James asked, alarm and consternation in his voice. Then he eased Patrick onto his back and saw the injury for himself.

Libby disentangled herself but stayed seated. "He's lost a lot of blood. The cut will need stitches."

After hasty introductions, Liam Kavanagh rescued the two backpacks from the mine. James and Dylan hoisted their injured sibling onto a portable litter and started back. Gavin gave her a weary smile. "I'm gonna piggyback you," he said. "It will be faster that way."

In the end, the trip through the forest took over two hours. The Kavanagh men had to be exhausted. It was four in the morning by the time they walked out of the woods and into the main lodge of Silver Reflections. Maeve was waiting for them, her face creased with worry.

The only brothers missing were Aidan, who, she learned, was out of town, and Conor who had gone to summon an ambulance. He'd kept his mother company during the rescue operation.

Maeve grabbed Libby into a huge hug. "Oh, my God. We've been out of our minds with worry." She bit her lip, eyeing Patrick's pale face as his brothers set the litter on a padded bench seat. "The ambulance is waiting."

Liam had radioed ahead to let Maeve know they were on the way.

In the hustle and bustle that followed, Libby found herself curled into a deep, comfy armchair by a fire someone had been kind enough to build in the middle of the night. When all the men disappeared, Maeve touched her arm. "Come on, sweetheart. I'll take you back to the hotel before I follow them to the emergency room. Are you sure you don't need medical attention?"

"No, ma'am. I'm fine."

Libby dozed in the car, waking up only as Maeve pulled up in front of Silver Beeches.

Maeve gazed at her, exhaustion on her face. "Do you need help getting upstairs?"

Libby knew her older friend was anxious to check on her son. "I'm fine, Maeve. Go see to Patrick. I'm going to bed as soon as I can get there."

Looking at her reflection in the bathroom mirror a short time later was a lesson in humility. Libby had seen corpses who had more color…and more fashion sense for that matter. Her clothes were filthy and torn, her hair was a tangled mess and, as an added indignity, her stomach rumbled loudly, making it known that sleep was going to have to wait.

The shower felt so good, she almost cried. After shampooing her hair three times and slathering it with conditioner, she used a washcloth to scrub away the grime from the rest of her body. She wove on her feet, fatigue weighting her limbs.

When she was clean and dry, she ordered room service. Six in the morning wasn't too early for bacon and eggs. She had every intention of cleaning her plate, but she managed only half of the bounty before she shoved the tray aside and fell facedown onto the soft, welcoming bed.

# Nine

Patrick wolfed down half of a sausage biscuit and watched as the female doc stitched up his leg. Thanks to several shots of numbing medicine, he was feeling no pain.

James leaned against the wall, as if guarding the room from unwanted intruders. Since they were the last people in the ER, Patrick was pretty sure any danger had been left behind at the mine. He and James had finally convinced all the others to go home and get some rest.

Patrick looked at his brother over the doctor's head. "Thanks, bro. You want to explain to me how you knew where I was?"

James's grin was tired but cocky. "I came up to Reflections yesterday to grab one of your gourmet lunches and see if you wanted to hike with me. The people at the front desk said you were in the forest teaching a new recruit the ropes. I set out around the mountain to catch up with you."

"You know where the campsite is…but have you ever even *been* to the mine?"

"No…but I've heard you talk about it. So I used my Boy Scout tracker skills and followed your trail. I eventually stumbled across the landslide. The mud was thick and slimy and fresh. It was then I realized you might be in trouble."

"Me and Libby…"

"Yeah. Since when do you camp out with pretty ladies?"

"It wasn't like that."

"I saw how she looked at you."

"We'd been through a tough time. It was a bonding experience." Patrick managed to keep his expression impassive, but his body was another story. "How did you dig us out?"

James grimaced. "That was the bad part. After I discovered I had *nothing* that was going to do the job, I ran back several miles to the knoll where we can usually get a phone signal and called Conor. He alerted everyone else. We all met up and brought the proper supplies."

"I owe you one, baby brother."

"Don't worry. I'll collect sooner or later. Like maybe an introduction to your newest employee?"

"I don't think so," Patrick snapped.

James raised an eyebrow. "Feeling a little territorial, are we?"

"She's not your type."

"Mom told me her story. She sounds like an amazing woman."

"She is. But she's had a tough time, and she doesn't need strange guys sniffing around."

"I'm not a strange guy… I'm your brother."

The doctor looked up from her work and smiled. "Do I need to referee this squabble?"

Patrick looked down at the long, red, angry wound on his leg. He hadn't needed a transfusion, but it was a close call. "No, Doc," he said, shooting his brother a glare.

Fortunately, Patrick's medical care wrapped up pretty quickly. In the car, James lifted an inquiring eyebrow. "Am I taking you home?"

Patrick gazed out the window, feeling exhausted and surly. "I want to go up to the hotel and make sure Libby is okay."

"She'll be asleep by now."

"Mom would give me a key."

James drummed his fingers on the steering wheel. "I know the two of you just spent the night together in a creepy, dark tunnel, but that doesn't give you the right to act like a stalker. Think, man. You can't open her door and peek in on her. That's way over the line."

Patrick slumped into his seat. His selfish need to see her would have to wait. "I guess you're right. Take me home."

After a shower, a light meal and five hours of sleep, Patrick found himself awake and antsy. The cut was on his left leg, so he wasn't limited as far as driving. When he couldn't stand being inside his house for another minute, he drove to Silver Reflections. His employees seemed perplexed to see him after his ordeal, so he holed up in his office.

Liam had left the two backpacks inside Patrick's door. Patrick dumped them out and started putting things away. One of the staff would take care of cleaning the tarps and other items. The rest Patrick stowed in specially labeled drawers along one wall of his suite.

When all of that was done, he couldn't wait any longer. He sent a text to Libby.

Hope you're feeling okay. You don't have to go Friday if you're not up to it. And stay home tomorrow...you deserve a rest...

He didn't dare say what he was really thinking...that he needed time to figure out what to do about her.

He hit Send and spun around in his leather chair. Maybe he'd been more affected by the experience in the mine than he realized, because his concentration was shot. When someone knocked at his door, he frowned, tempted to pretend he wasn't there.

But, after all, he was the boss. "Come in. It's open."

Libby was the last person he expected to see. She smiled. "I just got your text. Thanks for the consideration, but I couldn't sleep all day. I've been in my office talking to a guest who's disgruntled because he came here to relax and it's too peaceful to sleep. Apparently he lives in a brownstone walk-up across the street from a fire station."

"Ah. Maybe he needs more help than we can give."

"Maybe."

"I'm serious, Libby. Take tomorrow off. And do you still want to go to New York?"

"If you'll have me."

He would be damned glad to have her six ways to Sunday, but that wasn't what she meant. "You're welcome to come with me. As long as you know this isn't a nod from me about the job. I'll book you a hotel room this evening."

"Are you sure you want to do that? I've been learning how to manage on a budget. One room is definitely cheaper than two."

The challenging look in her eyes sent an unmistakable message. He stood up slowly and backed her against the door. "Are you sure it wasn't the adrenaline rush of certain death that sent you into my arms?" He kissed the side of her neck to test his hypothesis. His hips nudged hers. She was soft where he was hard.

Libby sighed as their bodies aligned with satisfying perfection. Her green eyes sparkled with excitement. "Perhaps it has escaped your notice, but you're a very sexy man."

"It was the bloody leg, right? Women can't resist a wounded hero."

"To be exact, I believe James was the hero."

She was taunting him deliberately. He knew that. And still, it pissed him off. "My brother is a great guy, but I doubt the two of you would get along."

"And why is that? I found him quite charming."

"If any Kavanagh is going to end up in your bed, it's going to be me." The declaration ended only a few decibels below a shout.

"Ooh…so intense. I have goose bumps. Still," she said, drawing the single syllable out to make a point. "I'm not sure it's a good idea to sleep with the boss."

"Then we won't sleep," he said. He kissed her wildly, feeling the press of her generous breasts against his chest. How had he ever thought she was meek and mousy?

Libby leaned into him, moaning when he deepened the kiss. "Your mother feels bad about our ordeal. She's treating me to a spa day and a shopping trip tomorrow. But I'll tell her no if you want me here. I'm not going to parlay this whole 'stuck in a mine' thing into special privileges."

"I *want* you to stay away," he said, entirely truthful. "I can't concentrate when you're around."

"How nice of you to say so."

He cupped her cheeks in his hands. "Be sure about this, sweet thing. If I do anything to hurt you, my mother will string me up by my ba—"

Libby clapped a hand over his mouth. "Watch your language, Mr. Kavanagh." She rubbed her thumb over his bottom lip. The simple caress sent fire streaking to his groin. "Are you *planning* on hurting me?"

He shifted from one foot to the other. "Of course not."

"Then relax and go with the flow. If nothing else in the last year, I've learned that's the only way to live…"

* * *

Libby took Patrick at his word about staying home the next day. She'd suffered no lasting physical effects from their unfortunate incarceration, but she *had* been tormented by dark dreams Wednesday night. She *needed* employment. But she *wanted* Patrick. Climbing into bed with him was not going to be in her best interests. The conflicting desires went around and around in her head. She woke up feeling groggy and vaguely depressed.

Maeve, however, refused to let any notion of gloom overshadow their day. When she met Libby in the lobby, she clapped her hands, practically dancing around like a child. "I'm so glad you're finally going to put your hair back to rights. I know your mother disliked that boring brown."

Libby raised her eyebrows. "Has anyone ever accused you of being overly tactful?"

Maeve chuckled, heading out to the large flagstone driveway where her silver Mercedes was parked. "I consider you family, my dear. And as your honorary aunt or stepmother or whatever you want to call me, I'm only doing my duty when I tell you that you have taken a beautiful young woman and turned her into a drudge."

Libby couldn't take offense. Maeve was absolutely too gleeful about restoring Libby's original looks. For a moment, Libby felt a surge of panic. She'd hidden behind her ill-fitting clothes and her nondescript hair color for the better part of a year. What if someone in New York recognized her?

As Maeve navigated the curvy road down the mountain, Libby took several deep breaths. She had started a new life. Did it matter if people knew who she was? *Libby* hadn't committed tax fraud.

Besides, most of the friends in her immediate social circle had melted away when the Parkhurst fortunes began to shatter. It was doubtful anyone would even want to acknowledge her. And as far as reporters were concerned, Libby Parkhurst was old news.

When Maeve found a parking spot in Silver Glen, the day of pampering began. First it was private massages, then manicures and pedicures at an upscale spa. Of course, most everything in Silver Glen was upscale. The beautiful alpine-themed town catered to the rich and famous.

An hour and a half later, once her Tahitian Sunset polish had dried, Libby admired her fingers and toes. This kind of self-indulgence had been one of the first things to go when she and her mother had been put out on the street.

It was amazing that something so simple could make a woman feel like she was ready to take on the world.

Next was the hair salon. Libby pulled a photo out of her wallet, one from her college graduation, and showed the stylist her original color. The woman was horrified. "Why would you ruin such an amazing head of hair? Never mind," she said quickly. "I don't even want to know. But before you leave here, young lady, I'm going to remind you what the good Lord intended you to look like."

Libby allowed the woman to whack three inches, since it had been ages since her last cut. Not only had Libby dyed her hair as part of her plan to go incognito, she had straightened it, as well. Little by little, the real Libby returned.

The stylist kept her promise. When it was done, Libby gazed in the mirror with tears in her eyes. Her natural hair was a curly, vibrant red that complemented her pale skin, unlike the dull brown that had washed her out and made her seem tired.

Now, the bouncy chin-length do put color in her cheeks. Parted on one side and tucked behind her ear on the other, the fun, youthful style framed her face and took years off her age.

Maeve beamed. "Beautiful. Absolutely beautiful."

Next stop was a charming boutique with an array of trendily clad mannequins in the window. Libby put her foot down. "I have money, Maeve. My first paycheck went in the bank this morning."

Patrick's mother frowned. "You nearly died in the service of a Kavanagh business. If I want to buy you a few things as a thank-you for not suing us, that is my prerogative."

Libby gaped. "You know I would never sue you. That's ridiculous."

But Maeve had already crossed the store and engaged the services of a young woman about Libby's own age. The clerk assessed Libby with a smile. "What kinds of things are we looking for today?"

Maeve shushed Libby when she tried to speak. The older woman steamrollered the conversation. "A little of everything. Casual chic. Business attire…not a suit, I think, but a little black dress. And a very dressy something for dinner…perhaps in ivory or even green if that's not too obvious with her fabulous hair."

The couture makeover became a whirlwind. Libby tried on so many garments, she lost count. When the frenzy was done, Maeve plunked down a credit card. "She'll wear the jeans and stilettos home…plus the peasant blouse. We'll take all the rest in garment bags."

Libby gave up trying to protest. In the months ahead, when she was able, she would do her best to repay Maeve. In the meantime, it was exciting to know that she would be able to accompany Patrick to New York looking her best.

Maeve declared herself exhausted when they returned to the Silver Beeches Lodge. "I'm going to see if Liam needs me," she said. "And if not, I'm headed home to put my feet up."

Libby hugged her impulsively. "Thank you, dear Maeve. I love you."

This time it was Maeve who had tears in her eyes. She took Libby's hands, her expression earnest. "Your mother was a precious woman…fragile, but precious. I still remember how proud she was when you were born. You were the light of her life. When you remember her, Libby, try not to think of the woman she became at the end, but instead, the woman she was at her best…the friend I knew so well."

Libby managed a smile. "It's no wonder your sons adore you."

Maeve waved a dismissive hand. "They think I'm a meddling pain in the ass. But then again, they know I'm always right."

Libby said her goodbyes and wandered upstairs to her room. She was determined to move to the apartment over the Silver Dollar saloon very soon. How many paychecks would it take before she could afford a rent payment? She chafed at the idea of living on Kavanagh charity, even if it was extremely luxurious and comfortable charity.

She and Maeve had lunched out before their appointments, so tonight, the only thing Libby ordered from room service was a chef salad. Often she ate downstairs in the dining room, but it had been a long, though pleasant, day. Sometimes it was nice to be alone and contemplate the future.

After her modest dinner, she packed the suitcase Maeve had loaned her. At one time, Libby had owned a wide array of expensive toiletries. Now she was accustomed to nothing more than discount-store moisturizer, an inexpensive tube of mascara and a couple of lipsticks for dressing up.

Her lace-and-silk nightgown and robe were remnants of the past. As were the several sets of bras and undies she possessed. It was one thing to sell haute couture at a resale shop. No one wanted underwear.

As she crawled into bed, she checked her phone. Patrick had messaged her earlier to let her know he would be sending a taxi to pick her up at seven o'clock tomorrow morning. They would rendezvous at the brand-new airstrip on the other end of the valley.

Patrick's brief text—and her equally brief response—was the only communication Libby had shared with him since she'd walked out of his office Wednesday afternoon. She missed him. And she had gone back and forth a dozen times about whether or not she was doing the right thing.

Their flirtatious conversation had left the status quo up in the air. What was going to happen when they got to New York?

She could tell herself it was all about finding closure… a bid for saying goodbye to her old life. And maybe trying one more time to convince Patrick she could do the job at Silver Reflections.

But she had a weak spot when it came to her fascinating boss. The possibility of sharing his bed made her shiver with anticipation. Right now, that agenda was winning.

# Ten

Patrick had decided to bring in one of the standby pilots the Kavanaghs sometimes used instead of flying himself. For one thing, the deep cut in his leg was still sore as hell. And for another, he liked the idea of sitting in the back of the jet with Libby. She was no stranger to luxury travel… so it wasn't that he wanted to see her reaction when he dazzled her with sophistication and pampering.

It was far simpler than that. He wanted to spend time with her.

He arrived at the airstrip thirty minutes early. The past two nights, he hadn't slept worth a damn. He kept reliving the moment the landslide happened. The instant Libby faced one of her worst fears. Because of him. Residual guilt tied his gut in a knot.

Not that she had suffered any lasting harm. Nevertheless, the experience in the mine was unpleasant to say the least. He never should have let her go down there.

He was already on the jet when the taxi pulled up. Peeking through the small window of the plane, he saw Libby get out. The day was drizzly and cold. She was wearing a black wool coat and carried a red-and-black umbrella, her face hidden. All he could see was long legs and sexy shoes.

The pilot was already in the cockpit preparing for take-off. Patrick went to the open cabin door and stood, ready to lend a hand if Libby needed help on the wet stairs. She hovered on the tarmac as the cabdriver handed a suitcase and matching carry-on to Patrick. Then she came up the steps.

Patrick moved back. "Hand me your umbrella." He'd been wrong about the coat. It wasn't wool at all, but instead, a fashionable all-weather trench-style, presumably heavily lined to deal with the cold weather in New York. A hood, edged in faux fur, framed her face.

For some reason, he couldn't look her in the eyes...not yet. "Make yourself comfortable," he said over his shoulder. After shaking the worst of the water from the umbrella, he closed it and stored it in a small closet. Then he retracted the jet's folding steps and turned the locking mechanisms on the cabin door.

"We'll be taking off in about five minutes."

At last, he turned around. Libby stood in the center of the cabin, her purse and coat on a seat beside her.

His heart punched once in his chest. Hard. His lungs forgot how to function. "Libby?" Incredulous, he stared at her. She was wearing a long-sleeve, scoop-necked black dress with a chunky silver necklace and matching earrings. The dress was completely plain. But the slubbed-knit fabric fit her body perfectly, emphasizing every sexy curve.

Even so, the dress wasn't what made the greatest impact. Nor was it the extremely fashionable but wildly impractical high heels that made her legs seem a million miles long. The dramatic jolt wasn't even a result of her darkly lashed green eyes or her soft crimson lips. It was her hair. God, her hair...

His mouth was probably hanging open, but he couldn't help it. He cleared his throat, shoving his hands in the pocket of his suit jacket to keep from grabbing her. "Whoever talked you into changing your color back to normal is a genius. It suits you perfectly." The deep red curls with gold highlights made her skin glow. The new cut framed her face and drew attention to high cheekbones and a slightly pointed chin.

Libby shrugged, seeming both pleased by and uncomfortable with his reaction. She and her mother had been harassed by reporters for months. Looking the way she did right now, it would have been impossible for her to fade into a crowd. Hence the metamorphosis from gorgeous socialite to little brown mouse.

She nodded, her eyes shadowed. "I've been hiding for a long time. But that's over, Patrick. I'm ready to move on."

He couldn't help himself. He closed the distance between them. "You're more than the sum of your looks, Libby."

"Thank you."

He winnowed his fingers through her hair. "It's so light…and fluffy…and *red*." He lowered his voice to a rough whisper. "I want to take you right here, right now. In that big overstuffed captain's chair. You make me crazy."

She looked at him, her soft green eyes roving his face, perhaps seeking assurance of his sincerity. "I want you, too, Patrick. Perhaps I shouldn't. My life is complicated enough already. But when I'm with you, I forget about all the bad stuff."

He frowned. "I'm not sure I want to be used as an amnesiac device."

"Don't think of it that way. You're like a drug. But the good kind. One that makes me feel alive in the best possible way. When I'm with you, I'm happy. It's as simple as that."

Her explanation mollified him somewhat, but he still wasn't entirely satisfied. He wanted to kiss her, but the pilot used the intercom to notify them of imminent take-off. "This discussion isn't over," he said.

They strapped into adjacent seats and prepared to be airborne. Libby turned to look out the window. Her profile was as familiar to him now as was his own. He struggled with a hodgepodge of emotions that left him feeling out of sorts.

He liked being Libby Parkhurst's savior. In the beginning he had resented his mother's interference. But once Libby was installed at Silver Reflections, it made him feel good to know he was helping make her life easier. Now that she had acquitted herself reasonably well in the woods, there was really no reason not to let her finish out Charlise's maternity leave.

But did he honestly want Libby under his nose 24/7? The situation would be perfect fodder for his mother's wedding-obsessed machinations behind the scenes. Patrick, however, was more worried about becoming a slobbering sex-starved idiot.

He had a business to run. Silver Reflections was doing very well, but any relatively new business had to keep on its toes. He couldn't afford to let his focus be drawn away by a woman, no matter how appealing.

The flight to New York was uneventful. Patrick worked on his presentation. Libby read a novel. They spoke occasionally, but it was stilted conversation. Was he the only one feeling shaken by what might happen during the night to come?

Libby felt like a girl in a fairy tale. Except this was backward. She had already been the princess with the world at her feet. Now she was an ordinary woman trying to embrace her new life.

It didn't hurt that Maeve had spoiled her with a suitcase full of new clothes. When Libby was growing up, her mother had bought Libby an entire new wardrobe every spring and fall. The castoffs were given to charity. They were always good clothes, some of them barely worn. Libby had never thought twice about it…other than the few times she had begged to keep a favorite sweater or pair of jeans.

Such excess seemed dreadful now. The clothes she'd brought with her this weekend would have to last several years. They were quality items, well made and classic in style. Perhaps Maeve was more perceptive than Libby realized, because during their wild shopping spree, Maeve had never once suggested anything that was faddish, nothing that would be dated by the next season.

On the other hand, Libby knew it wasn't the clothing that defined her new maturity. The past year had been a trial by fire. She had struggled with the emotional loss of her father, grieved the physical loss of her mother and juggled all of that alongside the almost inexplicable loss of her own identity.

And now there was Patrick. What to do about Patrick?

He disturbed her introspection. "Do you have any current plans to see your father?"

"Will you think I'm a terrible person if I say *no*?"

His smile was gentle and encompassed an understanding that threatened her composure. "Of course not. No one can make that decision for you."

She picked at the armrest. "I've sent him the occasional note. And of course, I called him after Mother, well…you know."

"Was he able to attend the funeral?"

"No. The request to the prison would have had to come from me, and I didn't think I could handle it. I was pretty much a mess. Fortunately, my parents had actually bought plots where my father grew up in Connecticut. They even prepaid for funerals. So at least I didn't have to worry about that."

"Has he written to you?"

"Only twice. I think he's ashamed. And embarrassed. But mostly angry he got caught. My father apparently subscribed to the theory that tax fraud isn't actually a crime unless someone finds out what you've done."

"He's not alone in that view."

"Doesn't make it right."

"How long does he have to serve?"

"Seven to ten. It was a lot of money. And apparently he was not exactly repentant in front of the judge."

"Time in prison can change people. Maybe it will show him what matters."

"I suppose…" But she was dubious. Her father was accustomed to throwing his weight around. His money had made it possible for him to demand *what* he wanted *when* he wanted. She had tried to find it in her heart to have sympathy for him. But she was still too shattered about the whole experience.

Patrick leaned forward and pointed out her window. "There's the skyline."

Libby took in the familiar sight and felt a stab of grief so raw and deep it caught her off guard. Patrick didn't say a word. But he used his finger to catch a tear that rolled down her cheek, and he finally offered her a pristine handkerchief to blow her nose.

"It's not my home anymore," she said, her throat so tight she could barely speak.

Patrick slid an arm around her shoulders. "It will always be your *first* home. And at some point, the trauma of what happened will become part of your past. Not so devastating that you think of it every day."

"I hope so."

"Silver Glen is a pretty good place for a fresh start. I know you came to the mountains to heal and to get back on your feet financially. My mother would be over the moon if you decided to stay forever."

"What about you, Patrick?"

The impulsive query came from her own lips, but shocked her nevertheless. It was the kind of needy leading question an insecure woman asks. "Don't answer that," she said quickly. "I don't know why I said it."

His expression was impassive, his thoughts impossible to decipher. "I have nothing to hide. I've already told you how I feel about marriage. I get the impression you're the kind of woman who will want a permanent relationship eventually. Maybe you can find that in Silver Glen. I don't know. But in the meantime, we've come very close to a line you may not want to cross when you're no longer in fear for your life."

"Don't patronize me," she said slowly. "I mentioned the one-hotel-room thing when I was safely out of the mine and standing in your office. Did you forget about that?"

"A relationship forged under duress doesn't usually stand the test of time."

She scowled, even as the plane bumped down on the runway at LaGuardia. "For a guy who's barely thirty, you pontificate like someone's grandmother."

He sighed, his jaw tight. "Are we having our first fight?"

"No," she snapped. "That happened when you called me a *misfit*."

"So many things are clear now," he muttered, his hot gaze skating from her lips to her breasts. "It's the red hair. I could have saved myself a lot of heartache if I'd known that the woman I interviewed in the beginning was not a mouse, but instead an exotic, hotheaded spitfire."

"Patronizing *and* chauvinistic."

A deep voice interrupted their quarrel. "Um, excuse me…Mr. Kavanagh? We have to deplane now."

Libby groaned inwardly, embarrassed beyond belief. How much had the pilot overheard? Grabbing her coat and shoving her arms into the sleeves, she scooped up her purse and climbed over Patrick's legs to head for the exit. He let her go, presumably lingering to deal with their luggage.

A private limo awaited them, a uniformed driver at the ready. When Patrick climbed in to the backseat with her, she ignored him pointedly, her face still hot with mortification.

How was a woman supposed to deal with a man who was both brutally honest and ridiculously appealing? Was she seriously going to settle for a temporary fling? And what was the time limit? When Charlise came back in six months, did the affair and the job end on the same day?

Patrick took her hand. "Quit sulking."

Her temper shot up several notches. She gave him a look that should have melted the door frame. "I've changed my mind. I want my own hotel room. I need a job more than I need you."

He stroked the inside of her wrist with his thumb. "Don't be mad, my beautiful girl. We're in New York. Alone. Away from my meddling family. We can do anything we want…anything at all."

His voice threatened to mesmerize her. Deep and husky with arousal, his words had the smooth cadence of a snake charmer. She shivered inwardly. "How easy do you think I am?" Her indignation dwindled rapidly in inverse proportion to the increase in her shaky breathing and the acceleration of her rushing pulse.

Patrick lifted her wrist and kissed the back of her hand. "You're not easy at all, Libby. You're damned difficult. Every time I think I have you figured out, you surprise me all over again."

She caught the chauffeur's gaze in the rearview mirror. The man lifted an eyebrow. Libby blushed again and stared out the window. "Not now, Patrick. We're almost there."

Patrick settled back in his seat, but the enigmatic smile on his face made Libby want to kiss the smirk off his face. Fortunately for her self-control, the car pulled up in front of their destination. While Patrick swiped his credit card, Libby slid out of the vehicle, shivering when a blast of cold air flipped up the tail of her coat.

"Where's our luggage?" she asked, suddenly anxious about Maeve's nice suitcases and Libby's new clothes.

"The driver is taking them on to the Carlyle. They'll hold them for us until check-in time."

He took her arm. "C'mon. We're early, but I want to make sure they're ready for us." Ushering her through sleek revolving doors, he hurried her into the building and onto the elevator. Fortunately for Libby, the small space was crowded, meaning she didn't have to talk to Patrick at all.

On the twenty-seventh floor, they exited. An eerily perfect receptionist greeted them. Behind her in platinum letters were the words *Peabody Rushford*. Libby took off her coat, using the opportunity to look around with curiosity. It was difficult to imagine anyone from this upscale environment insisting that executives participate in one of Patrick's field experiences.

Moments later, after a hushed communication via a high-tech intercom system, they were escorted to the boardroom where Patrick would do his presentation. Every chair at the glossy conference table was situated at an exact ninety-degree angle. Crystal tumblers filled with ice water sat on folded linen napkins.

Not a single item in the room was out of place. Except Libby. She felt ill at ease. Why had she agreed to accompany Patrick? Oh, wait. Tagging along had been her idea.

She was still holding out hope that she could convince him to give her the job.

The executives trickled into the room, first one or two, and then three or four, until finally, the entire team was assembled. Eight men, four women. Plus the graying boss. She guessed his *underlings* ranged in age from early thirties to late forties. Libby was easily the youngest person in the room.

Patrick greeted each participant warmly, introducing himself with the self-deprecatory charm she had come to expect from him. He was confident and humorous, and he interacted with both men and women equally well. When everyone was seated, there were three chairs remaining at one end of the table. Libby took the middle one, leaving a buffer on either side.

She was here as an interested observer. No need to get chummy. Not now at least. The future remained to be seen. If she continued to work for Patrick—and it was possible he might decide to let her stay on—then no doubt, she would be meeting these people in April.

Honestly, it was hard to imagine any of this crew getting dirty in the woods. The women wore similar quasi uniforms. Dark formfitting blazers with matching pencil skirts and white silk blouses. Their hairstyles fell into two camps…either sophisticated chignons or sharply modern pixie cuts.

The men were equally polished. Their dark suits resembled Patrick's. Though he wore a red power tie, the executives' neckwear was more conservative. Finally, the room settled, and Patrick began his spiel.

Libby knew Patrick was smart. But seeing him operate in this environment was eye-opening. He spoke to the group as an equal…a man with experience in their world as well as the master of his own domain, Silver Reflections.

As the orientation proceeded, Libby watched the faces

around the table. One of the women and several of the men were actively engaged, frequently asking questions… demonstrating enthusiasm and anticipation. Others exhibited veiled anxiety, and some were almost hostile.

Patrick had shared with Libby that the CEO was an ex-marine…a man both hard in business and in his physical demands on himself. For him to insist that his top management people participate in Patrick's program was asking a lot. Libby wondered if anyone would bail out, even if it might mean losing their jobs.

During the official Q and A time at the end, one of the quieter women who hadn't said a word so far raised her hand. When Patrick acknowledged her, she pointed at Libby. "Does she work for you? I'd like to hear what she has to say."

Patrick gave Libby a wry glance and shrugged. "Libby?"

All eyes in the room focused on her. She cleared her throat, scrambling for the right words. She would never forgive herself if she botched this for Patrick. "Well, um…"

The woman stared at her with naked apprehension. Clearly she wanted some kind of reassurance and saw Libby as a kindred spirit.

Libby smiled. "I certainly understand if anyone in this room, male or female, has reservations about spending a night or two in the woods, particularly if your personal history doesn't include campouts and bonfires. To be honest, I was the same way. But when I came to work for Patrick, it was important for me to try this *immersion* experience. I had to prove to myself that I could step outside my comfort zone."

The woman blanched. "And how did that go?"

Libby laughed softly. "I'll be honest. There were good parts and bad." No reason to go into the mine-shaft fiasco. "On the plus side, the setting is pristine and beautiful and serene. If you haven't been much of a nature lover in the past, I think you'll be one when the weekend is over."

"And the less wonderful parts?"

Though only one woman was doing the interrogation, Libby had a strong suspicion that others around the table were hanging on Libby's comments, looking for reassurance.

"Spending the night on the ground was a challenge, even with a comfy sleeping bag and a small pad. I'm a light sleeper to start with, so I found it difficult to relax enough to sleep deeply, even though I was tired."

"Anything else?"

Libby hesitated. Patrick grinned and nodded, as if not perturbed at all by anything she might have to say. "Well," she said, "there's the issue of using the bathroom in the woods. Women are always at a disadvantage there."

A titter of laughter circled the table.

Libby continued. "But all of this is minor stuff compared to the big picture. You'll learn to rely on teamwork to get simple tasks done like meals and setting up camp and taking it down. I think you'll see your coworkers in a new light. And I promise you that you'll find skills and talents you never knew you had. Patrick is not a drill sergeant. He's a facilitator. His knowledge is formidable. You can feel entirely safe with him in charge."

For a split second, the room was silent. Patrick was no longer smiling. If anything, he looked as if someone had punched him in the stomach. What was he thinking?

The woman asking the questions breathed an audible sigh of relief. "Thank you, Libby. I feel much better about this now."

The boss nodded. "I encourage my people to ask questions. It's the only way to learn."

Now some of the men seemed chagrined. Suddenly the woman in the group who had seemed like the weakest link had earned the boss's respect. Libby was pleased that her own small contribution had helped.

After the session adjourned, most of the staff returned to their offices. The boss lingered to speak with Patrick, expressing his opinion that the orientation had gone extremely well.

Then it was time to go. Patrick and Libby retraced their steps to the lobby, both of them quiet. Libby stood on the sidewalk, huddled into her coat. "Do we split up now? And meet at the hotel later?"

Patrick pulled up her hood and tucked a stray strand of hair inside. "Is it important for you to be alone when you revisit your old building?"

She searched his face. "No. Not really. But I assumed you had other things to do."

He kissed the tip of her nose. "My business is done. I'd like to take you to lunch, and then we'll face your past together."

"I might cry."

Patrick chuckled. "I think I can handle it. C'mon, I'm starving."

# Eleven

Patrick hailed a cab and helped Libby in, then ran around to the other side and joined her. Heavy clouds had rolled in. The sky overhead was gray and menacing. He gave the driver an address and sat back. "If you don't mind, Libby, I thought we would try a new place Aidan recommended. It's tucked away in the theater district, off the beaten path for tourists. He says they have the best homemade soups this side of North Carolina."

Libby smoothed the hem of her coat over her knees, unwittingly drawing attention to her legs. He had plans for those legs.

She nodded. "Sounds good, but I'm surprised. I thought men needed more than soup to consider it a meal."

"I might have forgotten to mention the gyros and turkey legs." His stomach growled on cue.

Libby laughed. "Now I get it."

"You were amazing back there," he said. "I never realized how much better these weekend trips would be if all the participants have the opportunity to calm their fears beforehand. Everything you said was perfect."

"But you've always done orientations…right?" She frowned.

"I have. Yes. But the dynamics of these high-powered firms are interesting. No one wants to appear weak in front of the boss."

"Then how was today different?"

"I think your presence at the table connected with that woman. She saw you as an ally. And perceived you to be truthful and sincere. So that gave her the courage to speak out. Truthfully, I think there were others in the room who shared some of the same anxieties. So even though they didn't *ask*, they also wanted to know what you had to say."

"I'm glad I could help."

Patrick glanced at his watch. "Now, we're officially off the clock…business concluded."

"There's a lot of the day still ahead."

He leaned over, took her chin in his hand and kissed her full on the lips. "I'm sure we can find some way to fill the time."

"I'll leave the planning up to you." Her demure answer was accompanied by a teasing smile that made him wish he could ditch the rest of the day's agenda and take her back to their room right now. Unfortunately, waiting wasn't his strong suit.

The change in her appearance still threw him off his stride. The Libby with whom he had communed out in the woods and down in the mine was spunky and cute and fun. He'd been aroused by her and interested in bedding her.

This newly revamped Libby was something else again. She made him feel like an overeager adolescent caught up in a surge of hormones that were probably killing off his brain cells in droves. His libido was louder than ever. *Take Libby. Take Libby. Man want woman.*

To disguise his increasing agitation, he pulled out his phone. With a muttered "excuse me," he pretended to check important emails. Libby was neither insulted nor overly perturbed by his distraction. She stared out the window of the cab, perhaps both pleased and yet anxious about revisiting her old stomping grounds.

That was one thing he loved about her. She wasn't jaded, even though a woman from her background certainly could be. Perhaps she had always been so fresh and open to life's surprises. Or maybe the places she and her mother had lived after being kicked out of their lavish home had taught Libby to appreciate her past.

The café where they had lunch was noisy and crowded. Patrick was glad. He wasn't in the mood for intimate conversation. His need to make love to Libby drowned out every other thought in his head.

Libby, on the other hand, chatted happily, her mood upbeat despite the fact that she was facing an emotional hurdle this afternoon.

He drank his coffee slowly, absently listening as his luncheon date conversed with the waitress about what it was like to be an understudy for an off-Broadway play. At last, the server walked away and Libby smiled at Patrick. "Sorry. I love hearing people's stories."

He raised an eyebrow. "Yet I haven't heard all of yours. What did you study in college? Who did you want to be when you grew up? How many boyfriends did you have along the way?"

A shadow flitted across her face. "I was an English major."

"Did you want to teach?"

"No. Not really. My parents wouldn't have approved."

"Too plebeian?" he asked, tongue in cheek.

Libby rolled her eyes at him. "Something like that."

"Then why the English major?"

She shrugged, her expression slightly defensive. "I loved books. It was the one area of study where I could indulge my obsession with the printed word and no one would criticize the hours I spent in the library."

"Is that what your parents did?"

Her smile was bleak this time. "They told me no man would want to marry a woman who was boring. That I should learn to entertain and decorate a house and choose fine wines and converse about politics and current events."

"Sounds like a Stepford wife."

"I suppose. It became a moot point when my father decided to defraud the government. My standing in society evaporated, not that I minded. At least not on my own account. I did feel very sorry for what it did to my mother. She never signed on for coupon clipping and shopping at discount clothing stores. My father spoiled her and pampered her, right up until the day he was carted away in handcuffs."

"That's all behind you now. Nothing but good times ahead."

He heard his own words and winced inwardly. What did *he* know about the struggles Libby faced? Even several years ago when he decided to give up his career in Chicago, it wasn't a huge risk. The Kavanagh family had deep pockets. He had started Silver Reflections with his own money, but if he had run into financial difficulties, there would have been plenty of help available to him. Never in his life had he faced the challenges that had been thrust upon Libby.

She wiped her mouth with a napkin and reapplied her lipstick. Watching her smooth on the sultry red color was an exercise in sexual frustration.

When she looked up, she caught him staring. He must have put on a good show, because she didn't appear to notice how close to the edge he was. Instead, she grimaced. "Let's go see my building before I get cold feet."

The sentence would have made sense, even if the words had been literal. The temperature outside had to have dropped at least ten degrees since they had arrived in the city.

He hailed another cab and looked at Libby. "You'll have to give the address this time."

"Of course." She nodded, her expression hard to decipher. But as they whizzed through the streets of the city, he saw her anxiety level rise.

When he took one of her hands in his, it was ice-cold. "Where are your gloves?"

"I didn't have any that matched this coat, and I wanted to look nice for your business associates."

"Oh, for God's sake, Libby. Here. Take mine." The ones in the pocket of his overcoat were old and well-worn, but they were leather, lined with cashmere. At least they would keep her warm in transit.

She barely seemed to notice his offering, but she didn't protest when he slid the gloves onto her hands. Finally, the cab stopped. "We're here," she said. For a moment, she didn't move.

"Libby? Are we going to get out?"

She looked at him blankly.

"Libby?" He kissed her nose. "C'mon, darlin'. There's no bogeyman waiting for you. Nothing but bricks and mortar."

"I know that."

Even so, when they stood on the sidewalk, she huddled against him, pretending to shelter herself from the wind. But they were shielded by the building, and the biting breeze had all but disappeared.

He put his arm around her shoulder, at a loss for how to

help her. "Which floor was yours?" he asked…anything to get her to talk.

"The penthouse. Daddy liked looking down on Central Park."

Patrick stood quietly, holding her close. "I'm here, Libby. You're not alone."

At last, she moved. He thought she meant only to walk past the impressive building, but she stopped in front of the double glass doors and, after a moment's hesitation, stepped forward to open them.

Before she could do so, a barrel-chested, white-haired man in a gray uniform with burgundy piping flung them wide. "Ms. Libby. Good God Almighty. I've been worried sick about you. I'm so sorry about your mother, baby girl. Come let me hug you."

Libby launched herself into the man's embrace and wrapped her arms around his ample waist. "Oh, Clarence. I've missed you so much."

Patrick watched in bemusement as the two old friends reconnected. He entered the lobby in deference to the cold, but hung back, unwilling to interfere with Libby's moment of closure.

At last, the old man acknowledged his presence. "Come on, Libby. Tell me about this handsome young fellow."

Libby blushed, her face alight with happiness. "That's my boss, Patrick Kavanagh. Patrick, this is Clarence Turner. He's known me since I was in diapers."

Clarence beamed. "Sweetest little gal you ever saw. And she grew up as beautiful on the inside as she was on the outside. For my sixtieth birthday, she made me a banana cream cake from scratch. Nicest thing anyone had ever done for me since my wife died."

Patrick stuck out his hand. "An honor to meet you, sir."

Clarence looked at Libby, his face troubled. "I'd take you upstairs if I could, but I think it would upset you. The new owners redid the whole place. You wouldn't recognize it."

"It doesn't matter," Libby said. "Seeing you is enough. I always thought my parents and I would give you a big, awesome gift when you retired…maybe a trip to Hawaii… or a new car. Turns out you'll be lucky to get a card and a pack of gum from me now."

She smiled and laughed when she said it, but Patrick knew it troubled her not to be able to help her old friend in any substantial way. Patrick made a mental note to follow up on the situation and see what he could do in Libby's name.

Clarence shot Patrick an assessing glance. "I thought maybe the two of you were an item," he said, not so subtly. "A man could do a lot worse than to marry Libby Parkhurst."

Before Patrick could reply, Libby jumped in. "Patrick and I are just friends. Actually, I'm working for his company temporarily. Patrick's mother and mine were good friends. Maeve Kavanagh has been helping me get back on my feet." She hugged Clarence one more time. "We have to go. But I promise to write more often. You're still at the same address?"

"Yes, indeed. They'll have to take me out of there feet-first." He looked at Patrick one more time and then back at Libby. "You're going to be okay, Libby. I never saw a girl with more grit or more light in her soul."

"Thank you for that, old friend."

When Patrick saw Libby's soft green eyes fill with tears, he decided it was time to go. "Nice to meet you, sir. I hope our paths will cross again."

Though Libby glanced over her shoulder and waved one last time as they braved the cold again, she didn't protest. Patrick had a feeling that the emotional reunion had taken more out of her than she realized.

On the sidewalk, he tipped up her chin and kissed her forehead. "How 'bout we go on the hotel and check in? I think we both could use a nap. If we're going to have a night on the town, you need your beauty sleep. And now that I think about it, I probably should get some play tickets."

They climbed into a cab and Libby took his hand. "What if we skip a play and just go out to dinner? That way we'd be back to the hotel early."

He swallowed, aware that the cabbie was perhaps listening, despite the fact that he had his radio on. "I'd like that very much." He clenched his other fist. "I want to be alone with you," he muttered.

"We could skip the nap, also."

In her eyes he saw everything he wanted and more. "I booked two rooms," he said hoarsely. "I didn't want to take advantage of you."

"I'm not weak, Patrick. I can take care of myself. And I was mad when I asked for that second room. We don't need it. I don't expect anything from you except pleasure."

"Pleasure?" His mouth was dry, his sex hard as stone. His brain had for all intents and purposes turned to mush.

She leaned into him. "Pleasure," she whispered. "You're a smart man. You'll figure it out."

Fortunately for Patrick's sanity, it was a brief cab ride. He paid the fare, aware all the while that Libby watched him.

He couldn't bear to look at her. He was too close to the edge.

At the front desk, the polite employee didn't blink an eye when Patrick canceled one of the rooms. The clerk dealt with the credit card and handed over the keys. "We've been holding your luggage, Mr. Kavanagh. I'll have it sent up immediately, along with a bottle of champagne and some canapés. Is there anything else we can do for you?"

Patrick swallowed, his hand shaking as he signed the charge slip. "No. Thank you."

He turned to Libby. "You ready to go upstairs?"

# Twelve

Libby linked her hand in his. "I'm ready." She was under no illusions. If she hadn't pushed the issue, Patrick might well have ignored the spark of attraction between them. He was wary of hurting Libby, and he had a healthy respect for his mother's good opinion.

Libby rested her head on his shoulder. They were alone in the elegant elevator. "No one will know about this but you and me, Patrick. You're not interested in a relationship, and I'm not, either. But that doesn't mean we can't enjoy each other's company."

His grip tightened on her hand when the elevator dinged. The bellman had come up on the service elevator, so there was a busy moment as Patrick opened the door and the luggage was situated. A second bellman came on the heels of the first, this one pushing a cart covered in white linen. The silver ice bucket chilled a bottle of bubbly. An offering of fancy cheese spreads and toast fingers resided on china dishes, along with strawberries and cream.

Once the efficient Carlyle employees disappeared, tips in hand, Patrick leaned against the door. "May I offer you a strawberry…or a glass of champagne?"

Libby nodded, her heart in her throat. "The latter please." She was accustomed to drinking fine champagne, but it had been a very long time. When Patrick handed her a crystal flute, she tipped it back and drank recklessly. The bubbly liquid was crisp and flavorful.

Patrick followed suit, although he sipped his drink slowly, eyeing her over the rim. "Have I told you how sexy you look in that dress?"

She was crestfallen. "I thought it was suitably professional."

"It *is* suitable," he said. "And professional. But the woman inside makes it something else entirely."

"Like what?" She held out her glass for a refill. Her knees were shaky. Was she going to chicken out now? She couldn't remember the last time she had experienced such genuine, shivery, sexual desire.

Patrick filled her flute a second time. But before he handed it to her, he took a sip…exactly where her lipstick had left a faint stain. "Tastes amazing," he said.

She kicked off her heels and curled her toes against the exquisite Oriental rug. Ordinarily, she hated panty hose with a passion, but the weather today had been a bit much for bare legs. There was no good way for a man to remove them…romantically speaking.

"Will you excuse me for a moment?" she asked, setting down her half-empty glass.

"Of course."

In the opulent bathroom, she covered her hot red cheeks with cold hands. She was going to have sex with Patrick Kavanagh. Casually. Temporarily.

Good girls didn't do such things. But then again, she'd

been a good girl for much of her life, and look where it had gotten her.

Rapidly, she stripped off her panty hose and stuffed them in a drawer of the vanity. She fluffed her hair and then held a damp cloth to her cheeks, trying to tame the wild color that was a dead giveaway as to her state of mind.

When she could linger no longer, she returned to the sitting room. It was lovely, with pale green and ecru walls. Antique French furnishings lent an air of romance. Patrick had even lit a candle, though it was the middle of the day.

He came to her and slid his hands beneath her hair, his smile holding the tiniest hint of male satisfaction. "Are you shy, Libby love?"

"Maybe. A little bit. I'm suddenly feeling rather unsophisticated."

"I don't want sophistication. I don't need it." His eyes had gone all dark and serious, the blue-gray irises like stormy lakes.

She curled her fingers around his wrists, not to push him away, but to hold on to something steady as her emotions cartwheeled. "What *do* you want and need, Patrick?"

He scooped her into his arms. "You, Libby. Only you."

On the way to the bedroom, he stopped to pick up the heavy pillar candle. But he couldn't manage it and Libby, too. Not without tumbling them all to the floor in a pile of hot wax. The image made her smile.

Patrick scowled. "Are you laughing at me?"

She looped an arm around his neck. "I wouldn't dare. I was merely contemplating all the ways I could use hot wax to drive you wild."

He stumbled and nearly lost his balance. His jaw dropped. Not much. But enough to let Libby know her little comment had left him gobsmacked. It felt good to have the upper hand, even if for only a moment.

The bedroom was something out of a fantasy…soft lavender sheets, fresh violets in a crystal vase…a Louis XIV chaise longue upholstered in sunshine-yellow and aubergine brocade. The ivory damask duvet had already been folded back. All Patrick had to do was gently drop Libby on the bed.

"Don't move," he said. "I'm going back for the ambience."

She barely had time to blink before he returned. He put the candle on the ornate dresser, a safe distance away. Then he closed the drapes, shutting out the gray afternoon light.

Libby propped her elbows behind her. "I thought you wanted a nap," she teased.

"Later," he said.

His jaw was tight, his cheekbones flushed. As he walked slowly toward the bed, he stripped off his tie and shirt and jacket with an economy of motion that was both intense and arousing…as if he couldn't bear to waste a single second. Libby's breath caught the first time she saw his bare chest.

"Nice show," she croaked. Her throat was dry, but the champagne was in the other room.

When he stood beside the bed, he unbuckled his belt and slid it free. Next went the shoes and socks. When he was down to his pants and nothing else, he crooked a finger. "Come here and turn around."

Trembling all over, she got up on her knees and presented her back to him. His fingertips found the top of her zipper and lowered it slowly. He cursed.

She looked over her shoulder, alarmed. "What's wrong?"

His expression was equal parts torment and lust. "You're too young. Too vulnerable. Too beautifully innocent."

"I'm not *entirely* innocent."

"I'm not talking about that kind of innocence," he said gruffly, stroking the length of her spine. He unfastened her bra, sliding his arms around her and palming her achy breasts. "It's *you*. All these things have tried to defeat you and yet you're still like a rosy-eyed child. As if nothing bad could ever happen."

She took one of his hands and raised it to her lips. "I'm only young in calendar years, Patrick. Life gave me an old soul, whether I wanted it or not. Now, quit agonizing over this and come to bed."

Patrick knew he was a lucky man. At this point in his life, he possessed most everything he'd ever wanted. But he had never wanted anything or anyone the way he wanted Libby Parkhurst. He wanted to be her knight, her protector, her one and only lover. The intensity of the desire overwhelmed him and left a hollow feeling in his chest. Because to have Libby in his life on a permanent basis would mean changes he wasn't prepared to make.

He wasn't in love with her. This was about sex. Nothing more.

He helped her out of the black dress. Underneath it, her bra and panties were pink lace. He'd never particularly been a fan of pink. But on her, it was perfect.

When she was completely naked, he sucked in a breath. "Get under the covers," he said gruffly. "Before you freeze."

He wondered if she saw through his equivocation. The room was plenty warm. But he needed a moment to collect himself. Turning away from the bed, he stripped off his pants and briefs. His erection could have hammered nails. He ached, almost bent over with the need to thrust inside her and find peace. When Libby flicked off the only remaining lamp, he turned around.

In the light from the single candle, her hair glowed like a nimbus around a naughty angel.

She curled on her side, the covers tucked to her chin. "I'm feeling nervous," she said quietly.

Did the woman have no filters? No emotional armor? "I'm feeling a bit shaky myself," he admitted.

Her eyes widened when she spotted the physical evidence of his excitement for the first time. "Really? 'Cause from over here it seems like you're good to go."

Her droll humor made him laugh. He flipped back the covers and joined her, his legs tangling with ones that were softer and more slender. "You have no concept of how much I want to make love to you."

"Why, Patrick? Why me?"

"Why not you?" He teased the nearest nipple, watching in fascination as it budded tightly.

"That's not an answer." She cried out when he bent to suckle her breast. But she must have meant for him to continue, because she clutched his head to her chest, her fingers twined in his hair.

She smelled like wildflowers and summer love affairs. In the midst of winter, she brought warmth and sunshine into this room, this bed.

He kissed her roughly. "Not everything in life can be explained, Libby."

Her arms wrapped around his neck, threatening to choke him. "Try."

"You give me something no one else ever has," he admitted quietly. "When I'm with you, everything seems right."

He saw in her eyes the recognition of his honesty. It wasn't something he planned. In fact, he felt damned naked in more ways than one. But if he couldn't give her forever, at least he could give her this.

"Make love to me, Patrick."

It was all he needed to hear and more. Later there would

be time for drawn-out foreplay and fancy moves. But at the moment, all he could think about was being inside her.

Reaching for the condoms he had dropped on the nightstand, he sheathed himself matter-of-factly, trying not to notice the way Libby's gaze followed his every motion. "Now, my Libby. Now."

He eased on top of her, careful to shield her from his entire weight. For a moment, he couldn't move. He was hard against her thigh, shuddering with the need to take and take and take.

Libby reached up and cradled his face in her hands. "I want you, too, Patrick."

"You wouldn't lie about not being a virgin…would you?"

Her eyes darkened with an emotion he didn't understand. "I don't lie about *anything*."

That was the problem. Few people in life were as transparent as Libby. If he hurt her, either physically or emotionally, he would know it. Immediately. Was he prepared for that responsibility? The first one, yes…no question. But the second?

Slowly, he eased inside her, pressing all the way until he could go no farther. Her sex was warm and tight. Yellow spots danced behind his eyelids. Every muscle in his body was tense.

Libby curled her legs around his waist, unwittingly driving him deeper still. "This is nice," she said, catching her breath.

"Nice?" He clenched his teeth. He was damned if he would come like a teenage boy—all flash and no substance.

Libby squeezed him inwardly, her mouth tipped up in a tiny smile that told him she enjoyed flexing her newfound power. "I give you high marks for the opening sequence. Very impressive delivery. Appealing package."

He choked out a laugh. "Haven't you ever heard of calling a spade a spade? You can refer to it as a co—"

She clapped a hand over his mouth with a move that was beginning to seem familiar. "No I can't."

"Where did you say you went to school?"

"Catholic everything. My parents were Protestant, but they liked the idea of surrounding their baby girl with nuns."

"Can we please not talk about nuns right now? It's throwing me off my game."

She nipped his chin with sharp teeth. "Proceed. You're doing very well so far."

When he flexed his hips, he managed to erase the smile from her face. "How about now?"

Libby tipped back her head and sighed, arching into his thrust. "Don't ever stop. What time is checkout tomorrow?"

The random conversation confounded him. As a rule, his bed partners were not so chatty. "Eleven. Twelve. Hell, I don't know. Why?"

Green eyes, hazy and unfocused, gazed up at him. "I want to calculate how many more times we can do this before we have to go home."

Libby was in deep trouble. She'd been lying to herself so well, she didn't even see the cliff ahead. And now she was about to tumble into disaster. Again.

At sixteen there had been some excuse. Not so much in her current situation.

Patrick was big and warm and solid, and that wasn't even taking into consideration the body part currently stroking her so intimately. He surrounded her, filled her, possessed her. The smell of his skin, the silky touch of his hair against her breasts. She could barely breathe from wanting him.

"Hush now, darlin'," he groaned, his Southern accent more pronounced as he ground his hips against hers. When he zeroed in on a certain spot, she cried out, her orgasm taking her by surprise.

The flash of climax was intense and prolonged, wave after wave of pleasure that left her lax and helpless in his embrace. But Patrick was lost, as well. His muffled shout against her neck was accompanied by fierce, frantic thrusts that culminated in his wild release.

When the storm passed, the room was silent but for their harsh breathing.

Coming back to New York had triggered an avalanche of feelings. And not only about her father's fall from grace. There was that other business, as well. The thing that still shamed her and made her question her judgment about men. She had never wanted to be so vulnerable again. But Patrick wouldn't hurt her, would he? At least not the way she'd been hurt before.

# Thirteen

Libby was having the most wonderful dream. She was floating in the ocean, the sun beaming down in gentle benediction. The temperature was exactly right. A warm blanket cocooned her as the breeze ruffled her hair.

Some sound far in the distance brought her awake with a jerk. Every cell in her body froze in stunned disbelief. Patrick Kavanagh lay half on top of her, his regular breathing steady and deep.

Holy Hannah. What had she done? Other than make it perfectly clear to Patrick that she was ready for dalliance with no expectation of anything more lasting than a weekend fling…

She eased out from under her lover, wincing when he muttered and frowned in his sleep. Fortunately, he settled back into slumber. He wasn't kidding about the nap. On the other hand, he probably needed it. The preceding week hadn't been a walk in the park. Maybe Patrick had experienced the same disturbing nightmares she had.

Caves with endless tunnels. Suffocating darkness. Musty air. Crypts and death. That's what came from having a too-vivid imagination.

Tiptoeing around the bed, she made her way into the other room and found her carry-on with her toiletry bag. Since she was naked as a baby at the moment, it also seemed prudent to locate her gown and robe. Patrick didn't stir when she quietly opened the bathroom door.

Once she was safely on the other side, she exhaled shakily. Nothing in the course of her admittedly limited sexual experience—much of it negative—had prepared her for Patrick's lovemaking. He was thorough. And intense. And enthusiastic. And generous. Did she mention generous? She'd lost track of her own orgasms. The man was a freaking genius in the bedroom. Who knew?

She wrapped a towel around her hair to keep it dry, and took an abbreviated shower. The thought of getting caught in the act was too terrifying to contemplate. The man had seen her naked. But that didn't mean a woman didn't like her privacy.

When she was clean and dry, she put on her silky nightwear. The soft ivory gown and robe were old, but still stylish and comfy. The fact that they were very thin gave her pause, but it was better than being nude.

Her hair did well with nothing more than a good brushing. Now all she had to do was pretend to be blasé, make her way through a fancy dinner and convince Patrick to sleep on the sofa.

She needed to put some distance between them. A barricade against doing something stupid. He'd already told her that marriage wasn't in the cards for him. Which meant this relationship was going nowhere.

If she let herself share his bed again, all bets were off. She might end up begging, and that would be the final indignity. He'd already called her a misfit once. She was sure as heck not going to let him pity her for crushing on him like a teenage girl.

She sat on the edge of the bathtub for ten minutes, trying to decide how to stage her return to the bedroom. In the end, Patrick took the matter out of her hands. He jerked open the door without ceremony and sighed—apparently in relief—when he saw her.

"I didn't know where you were," he complained.

The man was stark naked, his body a work of art. His *penis*—she could whisper that word in the privacy of her own head—hovered at half-mast, but was rapidly rising to attention. And apparently, the man had no modesty at all, because he stood there in the doorway, hands on hips, and glared at her. Not seeming at all concerned with his nudity. His spectacular, mouthwatering nudity.

"Where would I go?" she asked, trying not to look below his waist.

He ignored the question and strode toward her, dwarfing the generous dimensions of the bathroom. "I fail to see why you're wearing clothes. Aren't you the one who was doing mathematical calculations about potential episodes of sexual activity per hour?"

"That wasn't me," she lied, leaning back as his *stuff* practically whacked her in the nose.

His good humor returned. Without warning, he scooped her into his arms. "For future reference, no pj's unless I say so. And now that I think about it, no pj's at all."

Her cheek rested over the reassuring *thump-thump* of his heart. "These aren't pajamas. It's a peignoir set."

"I don't care if it's Queen Elizabeth's royal dressing gown. Ditch it, my love. Now."

He set her on her feet and, without further ado, lifted the two filmy layers over her head, ignoring her sputtering protests. "Patrick!"

He tossed the offending garments aside and ran his

hands from her neck to her shoulders, to her breasts, and all the way down to her bottom. "God, you're beautiful," he muttered.

"Oh, Patrick."

*"Oh, Patrick."* He mocked her gently. "Is that 'Oh, Patrick, I want to have sex with you again' or 'Oh, Patrick, you're the best lover I've ever had'?"

She caught her bottom lip with her teeth, torn between honesty and the need to keep his ego in check. "Well, both. But to be fair, you're only number two, so there's still room for comparison down the road."

His gaze sharpened. "Only number two?"

"I'm barely twenty-three."

"Yes, but a lot of girls are sexually active at sixteen."

"Not in my family. You do remember the nuns, right?"

"There you go again. Mentioning nuns at inappropriate moments. For the record, I knew one or two good little Catholic girls who taught me a lot about life. And sex."

Her eyes rounded. "Well, not me."

He thumbed her nipples, sending heat streaking all the way down to the damp juncture between her thighs. "You were amazing, Libby. Who taught you that thing you did there at the end?"

She shrugged demurely. "I read books."

"I see."

"You don't believe me?"

"You're awfully talented for a relative beginner."

The compliment was unexpected. "That's sweet of you to say."

"You want to tell me about number one?" Patrick seemed troubled, though she couldn't understand why.

She didn't. Not at all. The memory made her wince. "Maybe another time."

"Fair enough." He tipped his head and nibbled the side of her neck. "This will be slower, I promise."

She shuddered, her hands fisting at her sides. "I had no complaints."

Again, he scooped her into his arms, though this time he sat on the edge of the bed and turned her across his knees. "Do you have any spanking fantasies?"

She looked at him over her shoulder. "I can't say that I do, but feel free to test the hypothesis."

The sharp smack on her butt shocked her, even as the heat from his hand radiated throughout her pelvis. "That hurt, Patrick."

He chuckled. "Isn't that the point?"

The truth was, there was more to the sharp-edged play than hurt, but she didn't want to give him any ideas. She wriggled off his lap and knelt on the floor, resting her elbows on his bare knees and linking her hands underneath her chin. "I'll bet you know all sorts of kinky stuff, don't you?"

He grabbed handfuls of her hair and tugged gently. "Like the scenario where the desert sheikh takes the powerless English woman captive."

"I'm not English," she pointed out.

Patrick smiled tightly, sending a frisson of feminine apprehension down her spine. "We'll improvise. For the moment, let's see how you do on the oral exam. If you don't object, how about getting a washcloth and cleaning me up?"

"You mean so I can...?" Her voice trailed off. His erection bobbed in front of her. "Um, sure." She scuttled to the bathroom, painfully aware of his gaze following her progress. When she returned, he had leaned back on both hands. He didn't say a word.

But his challenging gaze tested her mettle. The balance of power was already unequal. He saw her as naive. Susceptible to being charmed by a man of experience. Though any and all of that might be true, she was determined to knock him off his feet.

Feigning confidence she did not possess, she sat at his hip and ran the washcloth over his intimate flesh, squeezing lightly. She smiled inwardly when he gasped, even though he tried to pretend it was a cough. "Too hard?" she asked, her expression guileless.

"No." Sweat beaded his forehead.

She continued to do her job, around and around, up and down. When she was finished, his flesh had turned to stone, and his chest rose and fell with every rapid breath.

Dropping the wet cloth on the floor, she bent, placed a hand on each of his thighs and took him in her mouth.

Patrick was pretty sure he had died and gone to heaven. He'd had blow jobs before. But none like this. His skin tightened all over his body. Libby's mouth was in turns delicate and firm. He couldn't predict her next move, and the uncertainty ratcheted up his arousal exponentially. He had promised her slow this time around, but already, he was at the breaking point. "Enough," he said, the word hoarse.

She looked up at him, her wide-eyed innocence no doubt damning him eternally for the lustful thoughts that turned him inside out. Putting his hands under her arms, he dragged her up onto the bed and kissed her recklessly. "Tell me what you want, Libby."

"I've never been on top."

*Sweet holy hell.* He swallowed hard. "Is that a request?"

She shrugged. "If you don't mind."

He took care of protection and moved onto his back. "You're in charge," he said, wondering if it were really true. He would hold out as long as he could, but the odds were iffy.

Libby seemed pleased by his gruff words. "I don't feel

very graceful," she complained as she attempted to mount the apparatus.

"The view from this side isn't bad."

When she slid down onto him without warning, he said a word that made her frown. "That's what we're doing, but you don't have to call it that."

She leaned forward, curling her fingertips into the depressions above his collarbone. "Don't you like this position?"

No one could be that naive. He gripped her firm ass and pulled her against him more firmly. "I've got your number now, Libby. You think you can drive me insane. But that's a two-edged sword. Wait until later when I tie your wrists to the bedposts and tickle you with a feather. You won't be so smug then, now will you?"

Her mouth formed a small perfect O. Her eyes widened. "Isn't that kind of advanced? We haven't known each other all that long. I think we should take things slowly...you know, get comfortable with each other before we branch out."

"I'm pretty damn comfortable right now." He put his hands under her breasts and bounced them experimentally. "These are nice."

She flushed. "Why are men so obsessed with boobs?"

"Maybe because we don't have any. I don't know. But you have to admit, they're beautiful."

"Now you've made me all weepy." Suppressing a smile, she leaned down and rested her forehead against his. "I didn't know it would be like this with you."

"Like what?"

"So easy. But so scary."

"I scare you?" He lifted her and eased her back down, making both of them gasp.

Without warning, she went for the dismount, nearly unmanning him in the process. She bounced off the bed and stood there, arms flung wide, her expression agitated. "You're ruining me for other men. I won't be able to find a husband after this."

He frowned. "I thought you were concentrating on rebuilding your life. That you didn't want a husband."

"Not today. Or tomorrow. But someday." She shook her head. "Now every guy I go to bed with is going to have to measure up to *that*." She pointed at his erection, seeming aggrieved by its very existence.

"You're overreacting. My co—" He stopped short. "My male *appendage* is perfectly normal," he said. "And people have casual sex all the time. Once we leave this hotel, it won't seem like such a big deal."

She folded her arms around her waist, apparently forgetting that she was bare-ass naked. "You know this from experience?"

"I have more than you, apparently. So, yes. And PS—it's bad form to walk out in the middle of the performance."

"I'm sorry." But she stood there so long he began to be afraid that she was actually going to call a halt to their madness.

He sat up and held out a hand. "Come back to bed, Libby. Please."

Her small smile loosened the knot in his stomach. "Well, if you ask that nicely…"

When he could reach her hand, he tugged, toppling her off balance and happily onto his lap. Libby sputtered and squirmed and protested until he flipped her and reversed their positions. Staring down at her, he felt something break apart and reform…a distinct seismic shift in his consciousness. Fortunately, he was good at ignoring extraneous details in the middle of serious business.

"Tell me you want me," he demanded.

"I want you."

"That wasn't convincing."

She linked her hands at the small of his back. "Patrick Kavanagh...I'll go mad with lust if you don't take me... right now."

"That's better." He shifted his weight and slid inside her, relishing the tight fit, the warm, wet friction. This was rapidly becoming an addiction, but he couldn't find it in his heart to care. His brain wasn't in the driver's seat. "I want you, too," he said, though she hadn't asked.

Libby's expressive eyes were closed, leaving him awash in doubt. What was she thinking? In the end, it didn't matter. His gut instincts took over, hammering home the message that she was the woman he needed. At least for now.

He felt the inner flutters that signaled her release. At last, he gave himself permission to finish recklessly, self-ishly. Again and again, he thrust. Scrambling for a pinnacle just out of reach. When the end came, it was bittersweet. Because he realized one mind-numbing fact.

Libby Parkhurst had burrowed her way beneath his guard. And maybe into his heart.

# Fourteen

"Hurry up, woman. We have dinner reservations in forty-five minutes."

Libby laughed, feeling happier than she had in a very long time. "I'll be ready in five." She leaned toward the mirror and touched up her eyeliner, then added a dash of smoky shadow.

After asking her preferences earlier in the day, Patrick had made reservations at an exclusive French restaurant high atop a Manhattan skyscraper. The evening promised to be magical.

She resisted the urge to pirouette in front of the mirror. The dress Maeve had bought for her was sexy and sophisticated and exceedingly feminine. The fabric was black lace over a gold satin underlay. The skirt ended modestly just at the knee, but the back dipped to the base of her spine.

Patrick rested his hands on her shoulders and kissed the nape of her neck, his hot gaze meeting hers in the mirror. "We could skip dinner," he said.

He was dressed in an expensive, conservative dark suit. The look in his eyes, however, was anything but ordinary.

She put her hand over one of his. "We need to keep up our strength. And besides, it would be a shame to waste all this sartorial splendor on room service."

"I could live with the disappointment," he muttered. He lifted the hem of her dress and stroked her thigh. "You can't go bare legged. It's cold outside."

"I thought you would be a fan of easy access."

"Maybe in July. But not tonight. I care about you too much to see you turn into a Popsicle."

Despite her distaste for the hosiery, she knew he was right. With that one adjustment to her wardrobe, she was ready. At least her black coat was fairly dressy. At one time she had owned an entire collection of high-end faux furs. But those were long gone.

Their cab was waiting when they got down to the lobby. It was dark now, and the wind that funneled between the buildings took her breath away as they stepped outside. Patrick didn't have to say, "I told you so." At least her legs had a layer of protection from the elements.

On the way, he played with the inside of her knee. "We could stay another night," he said.

The words were casual, but they stopped her heart. Because she wanted so very badly to say yes, she did the opposite. Too risky. She was letting him too close. "I don't think so," she said. "Your sister-in-law Zoe offered to help me move to Dylan's apartment Sunday afternoon, maybe find a few pillows and pictures to spruce it up. You probably remember she did a stint as a vagabond for a couple of years, so she has a good eye for a bargain."

"I see. We'll go back, then."

Had she wanted him to talk her into staying? Was she hurt that he dropped the idea so easily?

She didn't want to answer those questions, not even to herself.

They made it to the restaurant with ten minutes to spare. An obsequious maître d' seated them near the floor-to-ceiling windows at a table overlooking the city. Patrick tipped the man unobtrusively and pulled out Libby's chair.

"Does this suit your fancy?"

"Perfect," she sighed. The restaurant was new. And crowded. Discreet music filtered from hidden speakers overhead. Their fellow diners—men and women alike—dazzled in stunning couture clothing. Expensive accessories. Flashy jewelry. At one time, this had been Libby's life.

Patrick touched her hand across the table. "You okay?"

She shook off the moment of melancholy. "Yes. More than okay."

Another puffed-up employee, this one their waiter, appeared at the table. "Would Monsieur like to order for the lady?"

Patrick shook his head, smiling. "I don't think so."

Libby picked up her menu, and in flawless French ordered her favorite dish of scallops and prawns in cream sauce. The man had the decency to look chagrined before he turned to Patrick. "And you, sir?"

"I won't embarrass myself in front of the lady. Please bring me a filet, medium, and the asparagus in lemon butter."

"My pleasure."

When they were alone again, Libby grinned. "You set him straight, but so very nicely."

"The owners probably taught him that spiel. It's not his fault."

Libby gazed out the window, soaking in the vista of the city she considered home. "I don't think I'll stay in Silver Glen after this summer," she said impulsively. It would be impossibly difficult to be around the man who didn't want marriage and forever.

Patrick, caught in the act of sipping his wine, went still, his glass hovering in midair. "Oh? Why not?"

The reality was too painful, so she fed him a lesser truth. "I need to be independent. If I lean on your mom or even the Kavanaghs in general, I won't know if I really have the guts to rebuild my life. Here in New York, at least everything is familiar. I know the turf...and I have contacts...maybe even friends if I can figure out which ones still care about me now that my bank account is empty."

"So you don't see yourself becoming part of a place like Silver Glen?" His expression was curiously blank.

"I think we've established that I'm not much of a country girl. The concrete jungle is more my speed. I know which deli has the best pastrami, and I can tell you the operating hours of the Met and Natural History. I memorized the subway system by the time I was fourteen. I've seen the Rockettes dance every December since I was three years old...well, except for this past one. New York is home to me."

"I see."

His gaze was odd, turbulent. Did he think she was somehow insulting his beloved hometown?

"Don't get me wrong," she said hurriedly. "North Carolina is incredibly beautiful. And I'm happy to be living there for the moment. But when I think about the future, I can't see myself in Silver Glen."

In the heavy silence that followed her pronouncement the waiter returned, bearing their meals. The food was amazing, the presentation exceptional. But the evening had fallen flat.

She was honestly mystified. Patrick should be glad she wasn't going to hang around. He was the one with the matchmaking mother. And he'd made no secret of the fact that he was not ever going to get married.

For Libby's part, it made sense to decide from the beginning that she and Patrick were nothing more than a blip on the radar. She had suffered enough trauma in her life during the past year, without adding a broken heart to the mix.

Falling in love with Patrick Kavanagh would be the easiest thing in the world. Maybe she was partway there already. But she wasn't a fool. People didn't change. Her father hadn't. Her mother hadn't. And in the end, their inability to be the people they could have been desperately hurt their only daughter more than they could have imagined.

Still, Libby was tormented by one simple question. She knew she wouldn't be satisfied until she knew the answer.

Over dessert, she took a chance. "Patrick…"

"Hmm?" Distracted, he was dealing with the credit card and the check for their meal.

"May I ask you a personal question?"

He lifted an eyebrow, his sexy smile lethal. "I think we've reached that point, don't you?"

Maybe they had, and maybe they hadn't. But she risked it even so. "I know what happened to you when you were in high school. And I get that it was deeply painful and upsetting. But why have you decided that marriage is not for you?"

For a moment, he froze. She was certain he was going to tell her to go to hell. But then his shoulders relaxed and he sat back in his chair. "It's pretty simple really."

"Okay. Tell me."

"I've already done it. And messed it up. I choose not to take it so lightly again."

"I'm confused."

He fidgeted with his bow tie, his tanned fingers dark against the pristine white of his shirt. "Five of my brothers have gotten married so far. They've each stood in front of

God and family and made a solemn vow to one particular woman. To love and to cherish...till death do us part... all that stuff..."

"And you don't want to do that?"

"I'm telling you," he said, his voice rising slightly. "I already did it. But I cheapened the meaning of marriage. I bound myself to a woman, a girl really, whom I didn't love. And I knew I didn't love her even while I was repeating the vows."

"But you weren't an adult...and you were doing what was expected of you."

"Doesn't matter. The point is, I had my chance, and I made light of a moment that's supposed to be sacred. So I'm not going to take another woman in front of the altar knowing that I've already betrayed her before we ever start."

It made a weird sort of sense.

Poor Patrick...chained by the strength of his own regrets to life as a bachelor. And poor Libby...on the brink of falling for a man who didn't want anything she had to offer in the relationship department. It might have been funny if it hadn't been so wistfully sad.

Over one last cup of coffee, they sat in silence. Her question and his answer had driven an invisible wedge between them. She played with the silver demitasse spoon, watching the blinking lights far below...the traffic that never ceased. The Empire State Building off to her left was lit up, but the colors puzzled her. "I wonder why they went for pink and white this weekend," she murmured.

Patrick leaned forward. "Seriously? Tomorrow is Valentine's Day, Libby."

"Oh. Well, this is awkward."

"Why? Because you don't know what day it is?"

She lifted her chin. "No. Because you and I are the last two people who should be having a romantic dinner."

"Humans are good at pretense." The tinge of bitterness was unlike him.

But since her Cinderella experience was winding down, she chose to ignore his mood. She reached for his hand. "I don't want to fight with you, Patrick." She rubbed her thumb across the back of his hand. "Let's go back to the hotel. Please."

Patrick was not accustomed to self-doubt. He made decisions and followed through. He was mentally, physically and emotionally strong. People respected him...admired his integrity.

Then why did he feel as if he were failing Libby on every level?

He was so rattled by his jumbled thoughts that he forgot to call a cab before they got down to the street. "Stay inside a minute," he said.

But Libby had already gone on ahead, calling out to him with excitement in her voice. "Come look, Patrick. It's snowing..."

He followed her and pulled up short when the scene slammed into him with all the force of a freight train. Libby stood in the glow of a streetlight, arms upraised, her face tipped toward the sky. She was laughing, her features radiant. The sheltered heiress who had lost everything and been forced by harsh circumstances to grow up in a hurry, still had more joie de vivre in her little finger than Patrick could muster at the moment.

She had made love to him...openly, generously. Never once holding back or trying to protect herself from his *rules* for relationships. Even knowing that he was an emotionally locked-up bastard, she gave him everything. Her sweetness...her enthusiasm...her amazing body.

He should be kneeling at her feet and begging her forgiveness. Instead, he was going to commit the unforgivable sin. He was going to let her go.

As the snowfall grew heavier and the wind stilled, the whole world became hushed. Although he was miles from home, this particular gift of winter was the same everywhere. People stopped. Time stopped. Quiet descended. The swirl of white was an experience linked to childhood. Simple joy. Breathtaking wonder.

When he finally managed to hail a cab, he and Libby were coated in white. Strands of damp hair clung to her forehead, and her cheeks were pink. She laughed at him when he tried to brush the melting flakes from her shoulders. "Leave it," she said. "We'll be home soon."

He knew it was a slip of the tongue. A hotel, however lovely, was not home. But he was almost certain that Libby possessed a talent he lacked…the ability to make a real home with nothing more than her presence and her giving heart.

The trip from the cab to their suite seemed inordinately long. He shook, not from the cold, but from an amalgam of fear and desperation. This was it, most likely. His last chance to be with her intimately. His last opportunity to memorize the curve of her breasts, the softness of her bottom pressed to his pelvis as they curled together in sleep.

Libby's mood had segued from delight to quiet introspection. Perhaps she had picked up on the chaos inside him. But no matter the reason, she gave him space. Made no requests. He almost wanted her to demand something from him. To beg him to change. To plead with him to make an exception for her.

Libby, however, treated him like a grown man. She respected his choices, even as she made plans to go her own way. It was the most painful "letting go" he could have imagined.

As he fumbled with the key to their door, Libby slipped

her arm through his and leaned her head on his shoulder. "I think that last glass of wine was one too many," she murmured.

The door opened, and he scooted her through, backing her against it when it closed. His hands clenched her shoulders. His forehead rested against hers. "I need you." He meant to say more than that, but she understood.

She smiled at him as she unbuttoned her coat. "I know, Patrick. And it's okay, I promise. I won't ask for more than you're willing to give." She tossed the coat aside. "But we have tonight."

# Fifteen

He undressed her reverently, as if she were a long-awaited Christmas gift. Either Libby was very tired, or she understood his need to be gentle in this moment, because there was no mad stripping of clothes, no sex-crazed fumbling to get naked. With her head bowed, she submitted to his hands, even when those hands trembled and even when he cursed a stuck zipper.

At last, she was nude. He lifted her in his arms and carried her a few steps to the settee. Depositing her carefully, he stepped back and removed his own clothing. She watched him drowsily, her green eyes glowing with pleasure.

Her gaze was almost tactile on his bare skin. At last, it was done. He held out a hand. "Come with me."

That she obeyed instantly messed with his head. Was she trying to win him over? Or was she humoring a slightly deranged man who temporarily held her captive?

Did it matter?

As soon as she stood up, he recognized the possibilities in the elegant piece of furniture. "How do you feel about playacting the emperor and the concubine?"

"On someone else's furniture?" She was scandalized. "Not without something to protect it."

"Don't move." He raced to the bedroom and grabbed the blanket off the foot of the bed, along with a strip of condoms. When he returned, Libby had taken him at his word.

She stood, arms at her sides, and stared from him to the settee and back again. "I never took gymnastics classes. So don't get any kinky ideas."

"Kinky ideas are the best," he said. Teasing her was almost as much fun as making love to her. She sputtered and blushed and scowled adorably. Giving her a moment to get used to the idea, he flipped the thick duvet out and over the settee and sat down, palms flat on his thighs. "I'm ready."

Libby tilted her head to one side and pursed her lips. "Clearly."

"Well, come on."

"And do what?"

"Sit on my lap."

He watched as she assessed every possible permutation of that suggestion.

"Umm…"

"Don't be a chicken. You're a fearless woman who survived a night in the mine. Surely you're not afraid of a little role-playing."

"I'm not afraid of anything," she said firmly.

"I know it. And now you know it, too."

The look on her face was priceless. Libby had changed. She had grown. She was no longer the same woman who had professed timidity during her job interview.

"I don't know what to say. Thank you, Patrick."

He tucked his hands behind his head. "Don't thank me. You're the woman who has been slaying dragons."

She inhaled, making her breasts rise and fall in a way that would turn any man's brain to mush. "Okay, then…"

"Wait. Stop." He'd forgotten the protection. But, within seconds, he was sheathed and ready to go. "Come and get me."

"Isn't that supposed to be my line?"

He tickled the insides of her thighs as she gingerly straddled his lap. "I think an emperor would expect more bodily contact." He grabbed her butt and kneaded her warm, resilient flesh. "We should have a mirror," he complained, wishing he had been more prepared.

Libby cupped his neck with her hands and leaned in to kiss him. "Focus, Kavanagh. You have a naked woman on your lap."

"That's my problem," he complained, thoroughly aggrieved. "I forget my name when I touch you. It makes decision-making dicey at best."

"I'll help," she promised. "Give me something to decide."

"Well," he drawled. "It would be nice if you could get a little closer."

Fortunately, Libby was a smart woman. "Like this, you mean?" She lifted up and lowered, joining their bodies perfectly.

He buried his face in her scented breasts. "Exactly like that."

This particular position might have been a miscalculation. The visual stimulation combined with a somewhat passive role on his part made his body burn. He had barely entered her, and already he wanted to come.

*Damn it.*

But as much as he wanted to move, the urge was strong to simply hold her there. And pretend she was his to keep.

She tapped him on the head. "Hello in there. The last emperor who wanted me was a bit more…um…*active.*"

"You want active, little concubine?" he muttered. "How about this?" He surged upward, burying himself so deeply inside her, he wasn't sure he could find his way out.

"Patrick!" Libby cried out, stopping his heart.

"Did I hurt you?" he asked, pulling back to examine her face.

"You didn't hurt me." She bit her lip. "But it was definitely…"

"What? Definitely what?"

One shoulder lifted and fell. "Wicked. Memorable. Deep."

He swallowed hard. "I see. Would you consider those positive adjectives?"

She wiggled her butt, making him squeeze his eyes shut as he counted to ten and tried to hold on.

"Oh, yes, my emperor," she whispered. "Very positive indeed."

Libby might have lied a little bit. That last move on Patrick's part left her hovering on a line between pleasure and pain. She had never felt more desired, nor more completely possessed.

He trembled against her…or maybe that was her own body shaking. Was good sex always this momentous? Her basis for comparison was woefully inadequate. She'd had one terrible experience and now this one.

She raked her teeth along the shell of his ear. "Make love to me, Patrick. I want it all. Don't hold back."

Her request tore through his last thread of restraint. He lunged into her once…twice…then a third time, before he tumbled them both onto the floor and lifted one of her legs over his shoulder.

Suddenly, she felt exposed…vulnerable. Their bodies were no longer joined. Patrick was talented, but even he couldn't manage that trick while airborne. He stroked a fingertip in her damp sex, making her squirm as he stared at her intimately.

"Do you trust me, Libby?"

"Of course, I do."

"Close your eyes."

"But I…"

"Close them."

She obeyed the command, quivering in his grasp. "What are you going to do?"

"Hush, Libby."

She sensed him moving, and then she arched her back in instinctive protest when she felt his hands spread her legs apart. Moments later, his warm breath gave her the first warning of what he was about to do seconds before she felt the rough pass of his tongue on her sex.

A groan ripped from her gut, shocked pleasure swamping her inhibitions. She tried to escape, even so. But he locked her legs to the rug and continued his lazy torture.

She came more than once…loudly. And in the end, she barely had the breath to whisper his name when he moved inside her and drove them both insane…

It was still dark when Libby awoke. She was sore and satiated but oddly uncertain. Some sound had dragged her from a deep sleep. Patrick breathed quietly at her back, his arms wrapped around her waist, his face buried in her hair.

"Patrick," she said, turning to face him. "I think your phone is vibrating." It had to be bad. No good news ever came at…what was it? Four in the morning?

Her companion grumbled, but reached for his phone on the bedside table. "What?"

Patrick sat straight up in bed. "How bad is it?"

The tone in his voice alarmed her. "What's wrong?"

He ignored her until he finished the call. "It's Mia…

Dylan's wife. She's in the hospital with a ruptured appendix. And there are complications."

"Oh, no..."

"There's nothing we can do to help."

"Are you trying to convince me or you? Come on, Patrick. You know we need to go back. At least we can be there to lend moral support. People die from a ruptured appendix sometimes. Dylan must be out of his mind."

"Thank you for understanding," he said quietly.

They barely spoke as they gathered up their things and dressed. Patrick hardly acknowledged Libby's presence. She forgave him his silence, though, because she knew what it was like to be sick with fear.

A car waited for them when they exited the hotel. Apparently nothing ruffled the overnight desk clerk, even guests rushing out with their hair askew and wearing rumpled clothing from the night before.

At the airport, the pilot was ready. The flight back to Silver Glen seemed endless. Patrick stared out the window. Libby dozed. By eight in the morning, they were touching down on the new airstrip.

James was waiting for them, the car warm and toasty, despite the frigid early-morning air. As James stowed their bags into the trunk, Patrick helped Libby into the backseat and then joined James up front.

"How is she?" Patrick asked. "And tell me what happened. I didn't wait for details earlier when Liam contacted us."

James grimaced. "Apparently, she started having severe pain sometime after midnight, but she didn't wake up Dylan, because she didn't want to have to get Cora out of bed. By three thirty, it was so bad she had no choice. Dylan didn't take her. She went by ambulance. She's in surgery right now."

"Damn it, women are stubborn."

"Yeah."

Libby stayed silent in the backseat, hearing the concern in the siblings' voices…and the faintest hint of panic. These were big strong men. But they loved their sisters-in-law and treated them as blood relations, integral parts of this large, tight-knit family.

At the hospital, Libby staked out a seat in the waiting room and tried to become invisible. Through the glass walls adjacent to the corridor she had seen Maeve, the brothers and most of their wives from time to time, pacing the halls. Still wearing her coat to cover her inappropriate clothing, Libby closed her eyes and leaned her head against the wall. This setting brought back too many painful memories of her mother's early suicide attempts.

When Patrick finally sought her out, almost two hours had elapsed. He plopped down in a chair across from her and rested his elbows on his knees, head in his hands. Wearing his tux pants and wrinkled white shirt, he looked exhausted.

"Patrick?" Alarm coursed through her veins. "Did something go wrong? Is Mia okay?"

He sat up slowly, his expression taut with stress. "She's going to be. At least I hope so. The surgery went well, but infection is a concern. She was in recovery for forty-five minutes. They've brought her up to a room now. We've been taking turns going in to see her."

"How is she?"

"Cranky at the moment. She hates being out of control."

"I'm sure it's scary for her."

"Yeah." He pushed his hair from his forehead, his eyes weary, but laden with something else, as well. "Dylan is an absolute wreck."

At that moment, Maeve walked into the waiting room. Normally, Patrick's mother was the epitome of vigor and elegance, never a hair out of place. This morning, however, she looked every bit her age.

Patrick jumped up. "Here. Take my seat, Mom. I'm going to find some coffee."

Maeve managed a smile, but her hands trembled as she sat down and looked at Libby. "It's a hard thing to watch your children suffer. My poor Dylan is stoic, but I was afraid he was going to have a heart attack. He loves Mia deeply. And I do, too, of course. A man's love for his wife, though, is a sacred thing."

"I'm so glad it looks like Mia is going to be okay."

"Would you mind driving me home, dear? I told Patrick I was going to ask you. He's already had your things sent up to the lodge."

"Are you okay, Maeve?" The older woman was definitely pale.

Maeve nodded. "I'm fine. Just a little shaky, because I never ate breakfast. My car is in the parking lot."

They made their way downstairs, pausing to speak to various members of the family. But Patrick had not returned. As they exited the hospital, Libby's stomach growled. "Would you like to stop at the diner for a meal?"

"Actually, that sounds wonderful. Thank you, dear."

The little restaurant wasn't crowded. Maybe because it wasn't a weekday. Libby and Maeve grabbed a booth and ordered bacon and eggs with a side of heart-shaped pancakes in honor of the holiday. Coffee and orange juice came out ahead of the food. Libby drained her cup in short order, hoping the jolt of caffeine would kick in soon. Maeve did the same, but she eyed Libby over the rim.

"I'm glad you suggested breakfast, Libby. I wanted to ask how the New York weekend went. I see you're still wearing that lovely dress."

Libby drew the collar of her coat closer together, thankful that the temperatures justified her attire. "We left in such a hurry this morning, we both just grabbed our clothes from last night."

Maeve's smile was knowing. "I wasn't making a judgment call…merely commenting. So tell me…did things go well?"

"The orientation at Peabody Rushford was fascinating. Although it wasn't for *my* benefit, I learned a lot."

Maeve shook her head, her dark eyes sharp with interest. "I'm not really asking about Patrick's business dealings. My son is an astute entrepreneur. I would expect no less. Mine was a more personal question."

Most people wouldn't have the guts to pry. But Maeve was not most people. Libby could do nothing about the flood of heat that washed from her throat to her hairline. "I'm not sure what you mean."

The server delivered the food. Libby scooped a forkful of eggs, hoping the distraction would derail Maeve's interrogation.

But Patrick's mother was like a dog with a bone… a very tasty bone. "I don't expect a blow-by-blow description, but I would like to know if the two of you connected on an intimate level." She locked her steady gaze with Libby's flustered one.

*Blow-by-blow? Good grief.* Libby managed to swallow the eggs that had solidified into a lump in her throat. "Um…yes, ma'am. We did."

"But?"

"But what?"

"You hardly seem the picture of a young woman who has been swept off her feet by romance."

"I haven't had much sleep, Maeve. It's a long way from New York."

"Give Patrick a chance," Maeve begged. "I know he doesn't go in for big gestures and declarations of undying passion, but he's a deep man. You can unpeel the layers if only you'll be patient."

Libby reached across the table and took Maeve's hand, squeezing it for a moment. Then she sat back in the booth and sighed. The delicious breakfast had lost its appeal. "Patrick is an *amazing* man. But he's been very honest with me from the beginning, and I have to honor that. For you to interfere or for me to weave daydreams based on nothing at all, would be wrong."

Maeve's face fell. "But you care about him?"

"Of course I do. He's a lovely man. But that doesn't make us soul mates, Maeve."

"I don't want my son to spend his life alone."

Tears glistened in Maeve's eyes. Given Patrick's mother's talents for benign manipulation, Libby had to wonder if the tears were genuine. But then again, Maeve was capable of deep feeling. Everything she did came from a place of abundant love.

"Some people like being alone, Maeve. I know tons of single people who are very happy and content with their lives. Patrick has a rewarding career and a circle of intimate friends. You can't box him into a *relationship* corner he doesn't want or need."

"You sound awfully wise for a young woman of your age."

"Life is a tough teacher."

"So what you're telling me is that you won't even consider letting yourself fall in love with my son because he's told you he doesn't want to get married."

"That's about the sum of it. I may stay for the duration of Charlise's leave…as long as things don't get awkward. But I've already told Patrick that I'm thinking of going back to New York permanently. This weekend's trip told me I can handle it. I wasn't sure, to be honest. I didn't want to think about my mother's death and my father's crime every second of every day. But I think it's going to be okay."

"Well…" Maeve scowled at a strip of bacon. "It sounds like you know your own mind."

"Yes, ma'am. And don't worry about Patrick. He knows what he wants and what he doesn't want."

Maeve leaned forward. "So what *does* he want?"

"He wants to build his life here…among family. He wants to be close to you and his brothers, and their wives and children, both physically and emotionally. He wants to grow Silver Reflections and know that he's making a difference in people's lives. He wants to spend time in the mountains and to draw strength from this place you all call home."

"For a woman who hasn't found her soul mate, you surely sound as if you know a great deal about my son."

"Stop it, Maeve. I'm serious. This last year has taught me that I can't always bend the world to my will. I have to accept reality and deal with it as best I can. And even under those circumstances—sometimes difficult, sometimes tragic—I can be happy. Or at least content."

Maeve held up her hands. "You've convinced me. I'm officially done with playing Cupid…though it's awfully hard to say that on his special day."

Libby laughed, finishing her meal with a lighter heart. "Maybe *we* should be worrying about *you*, Maeve. You're still very youthful and attractive. I'm sure there are tons of eligible men out there who would like to find a woman like you."

Maeve blanched. "If that's blackmail, I stand forewarned. I like my life the way it is. I had one husband. That was enough."

"If you say so. Now please pass the syrup, let's finish breakfast so I can go back to the lodge and get out of these clothes."

# Sixteen

Patrick kicked a log, not even flinching when pain shot from his toe up his leg. He liked the pain. It helped distract him from the turmoil in the rest of his body. It had been over twenty-four hours since he had seen Libby. Longer than that since they'd had sex. He was like a junkie jonesing for the next hit.

But therein lay his problem. He had to stay away from her.

The conviction had been born in an intimate New York hotel room and solidified in the antiseptic corridors of a hospital. He couldn't afford to fall in love with Libby Parkhurst. It was too dangerous.

Little memories of Friday slipped into his thoughts when his guard was down. The smell of her hair on his pillow. The humorous, self-deprecating way she spoke to his clients about sleeping in the great outdoors. Her delighted laughter as she tipped her face toward the sky while snowflakes fell on her soft cheeks.

Even the way she hugged an old man in a uniform and let him know that he was important in her life.

Libby made everything brighter, more special. If he'd been inclined to find a lover and hang on to her, that woman might be Libby. But he couldn't. He wouldn't.

Without realizing it, he'd been on his way to changing his life plan. Having Libby in his bed, turning him inside out, had begun to convince him that he might be smarter about marriage a second time. After all, he wasn't a kid anymore.

But then yesterday happened. Mia's emergency surgery. Patrick knew his brother Dylan as a laid-back, comfortable-with-the-world, confident man. But in Dylan's eyes yesterday, Patrick had seen raw terror. With the woman Dylan loved in danger, Patrick's older brother had been helpless... scared sick that he was going to lose his whole world.

Patrick didn't want that kind of responsibility or that kind of grief. He remembered well the bitter taste of failure and loss when his youthful marriage ended, and that was for a girl he hadn't even loved.

How much worse would it be if he let himself get addicted to Libby and then he lost her? Death. Divorce. Infidelity. There were any number of forces waiting to tear couples apart.

Why would he subject himself to such vulnerability?

The hours he'd spent with Libby in the Carlyle hotel had literally changed him. Her sweet, sultry beauty. Her gentleness. Her shy, eager passion. He could have wallowed in their lovemaking for days on end and never had enough.

But when he broached the subject of extending their stay, Libby hadn't jumped at the idea. Worse still, she'd spoken of returning to New York permanently. Of leaving Silver Glen. Of leaving him.

It wasn't too late to correct his mistakes. He hadn't

gone all the way into obsession. He could end this thing and walk away unscathed.

But to do so meant suffering through one very unpleasant conversation. Today was Sunday. Thank God, Valentine's Day had come and gone. There was no reason not to intercept Libby's plans before she returned to Silver Reflections Monday morning.

When he contemplated what he was about to do, the bottom fell out of his stomach. Much like the first time he'd stood atop the high dive as a ten-year-old and wondered if he had the guts to make the jump.

He took out his cell phone and started to punch in a number. Libby carried a cheap pay-as-you-go phone. But at the last minute he remembered that Zoe was helping Libby get set up in the apartment over Dylan's bar.

The two of them had vowed to hit up thrift stores and outfit Libby's new digs. Should he stop Libby before she spent any of her hard-earned cash on things she might not need?

Damn it. He'd never had to deal with any of this with Charlise at his side.

At last, he decided he had to make the call.

Libby answered on the first ring. "Hello?"

Her voice reached inside his chest and squeezed his heart. "Are you and Zoe still occupied with your move?"

"She had to cancel. But I may go over to the Silver Dollar later to get the lay of the land. What's up, Patrick?"

"We need to talk," he said gruffly. "What if I pick up some sandwiches, and you and I go for a drive?"

"It's not really picnic weather," she said, laughter in her voice.

The day was infinitely dreary, sheets of rain drenching the mountains, temperatures hovering at a raw 38 degrees.

"I know that," he said. "But I've eaten in my car before. It won't kill me."

"If you say so."

"Can you be ready in an hour?"

"Of course."

"See you shortly." Now that he had made up his mind, he wanted to get this thing done...

Libby had a good idea what was coming. Patrick was going to tell her that an intimate relationship was not a good idea since she was going to be working for him. The thing was, she sort of agreed.

At this point in her life, she needed a good job more than she needed a love interest. Maybe in time this physical attraction between the two of them might blossom into something stronger...something lasting. She was a patient person. And if that were never going to happen, then she would be a big girl and face the truth.

Despite her brave talk, the prospect of seeing Patrick again made her insides go wobbly. They had gone from sleeping in each other's arms, to panic, to rushed travel to the hospital, to nothing. Patrick had left to get coffee, and that was the last she had seen of him.

This afternoon, with one guarded phone call, he was evidently prepared to set her straight. A fling in New York was one thing. Now it would be back to business as usual.

Since they weren't going anywhere fancy, she dressed warmly in jeans, boots and a thick, forest green sweater. The pleasant weather when Patrick had taken her out in the woods was nothing but a memory. Winter had returned... with no sign of relenting.

She was waiting on the front steps of the hotel when Patrick pulled up in his sporty sedan. It didn't seem like a good idea to meet him inside where his mother might happen to see them and get the wrong idea.

Ever the gentleman, he got out and opened her door, despite the fact that a uniformed parking attendant stood nearby, ready to lend a hand. She wanted to smile at Patrick and say something light and innocuous, but the words dried up in her throat.

This man had seen her naked. He had done wonderfully wicked things to her and with her. They had slept like exhausted children, wrapped in each other's arms.

Looking at Patrick's stoic face right now, no one would ever guess any of that.

Once they were seated practically hip to hip in the interior of the car, things got worse. The windows fogged up and the tension increased exponentially. She literally said nothing.

Patrick followed her lead.

She wanted to ask where they were going. But Patrick's grim profile in the waning afternoon light didn't invite questions. Chastened, she huddled in her seat and watched as the world flew by her window.

He drove like a man possessed, spiraling down the mountain road at least ten miles above the speed limit, and then racing on past town and out into the countryside. If he had a destination, she couldn't guess what it was. Her gut said he was driving at random.

When thirty minutes had passed from the moment he fetched her at the lodge, he finally slowed the car and rolled to a stop. The scene spread out in front of them was the definition of *middle of nowhere*. If she hadn't known better, she might have been worried he was going to dump her out and drive away, leaving her to find her way back home.

Their meal was in the backseat, but she wasn't hungry. And since she'd never been one to put off unpleasant tasks, she decided to cut to the chase. "I've been expecting this conversation," she said quietly. "You're going to say that we can either be lovers or coworkers, but not both."

Patrick's hands were white-knuckled on the steering

wheel. "The rain has stopped. I need to get out of this car. Do you mind?"

His question was clearly rhetorical, because before she could respond, he had already climbed out. She joined him on the side of the road, her arms wrapped around her waist. Even with a coat over her sweater, she was cold. The graveled edges of the pavement were waterlogged and muddy. The tops of the surrounding mountains were invisible, shrouded in low clouds, though the sun was trying to peek through.

Patrick stood a few feet away, physically and emotionally aloof, with aviator sunglasses obscuring part of his face. His khakis were crisply creased. He wore a white shirt underneath a brown bomber jacket. The leather was soft and scarred, clearly the real deal. Who had given it to him? Maybe it had been a gift when he first earned his pilot's license.

A light breeze ruffled his hair. Though she couldn't see his eyes, she guessed they were more gray than blue in this light. "Are you asking *me* to decide? New York was incredible, Patrick. I want to pick sex with you and say to hell with everything else. But we don't know each other all that well, and I was serious about learning to stand on my own two feet."

"You've misunderstood me," he said, hands shoved in his pocket.

"Does that mean *you* get to choose? I have no say in the matter?"

His expression was grim, his jaw so tight he would surely have a headache soon if he didn't already. It wasn't the face of a man who was going to choose physical pleasure over their work relationship.

He held up a hand. "Stop, Libby." His voice was hoarse. "You're making this harder."

Disappointment set up residence in her stomach.

Clearly the sex that had seemed so incredibly intimate and warm and fun to her had meant nothing to him. Well, she wouldn't be an object of pity. If he thought she was going to pine away for him, he was wrong. As far as she was concerned, they could work together and pretend the past weekend never happened.

She mimed zipping her lip. "Say what you have to say."

He took off his sunglasses and tucked them in his pocket. In the battle between the clouds and the sun, the clouds had won. "I'm not asking you to choose, Libby. I think you were right. You should go back to New York."

Trembling began deep in her core and worked its way to her extremities. "I don't understand."

In his face, she saw no remnant of the tender, funny man who had made love to her so passionately and so well. He stared at her impassively. "You gave it your best shot, Libby. I admired your resolve in the woods and in the mine, but you're not who I need while Charlise is gone."

*You're not who I need.* The blunt statement took her breath away.

"And our physical relationship?" Now her entire body shook. She tightened her arms around herself, trying not to splinter into a million tiny pieces of disbelief and wounded embarrassment.

"One night does not make a relationship. We were great in bed, but I've already told you how I feel about marriage. If you stay in Silver Glen, and you and I *continue* to end up in bed, things will get messy.

*"Messy..."* She parroted the word, her thought processes in shambles.

"You have to go home, Libby. Your instincts were good about that. Silver Glen is not the place for you, and I'm not the man you want. It's better to put an end to this now with no harm done."

Somewhere, she found the strength to smile evenly,

even as jagged, breathless pain raced through her veins and threatened to cripple her. It was a hell of a time to realize she was in love with him. She inhaled and exhaled, calling upon all of her acting skills. "I can't say I'm surprised by your decision. I never really thought you were going to give me the job anyway."

He must have seen through her layer of calm. For the first time, something in him cracked...visibly. For a split second, she could swear she saw agony in his eyes. "Libby..." He took an impulsive step in her direction and reached for her arm.

She jerked away, backing up so quickly she nearly lost her footing in the loose gravel. "No. Just no. Please take me back to the hotel. I have plans to make."

The return drive seemed endless. In front of the Silver Beeches Lodge, Patrick rolled to a halt and locked all the car doors with one click. His chest heaved. "Libby..." he said her name again.

But his time she had no escape route. He leaned across the console and tangled his hands in her hair, pulling her to him for a hard, desperate kiss. It took guts and fortitude, but she didn't respond. At all.

When he finally released her and sat back, she slapped him hard across the face. In seconds, his cheek bore the dark red mark of her fingers. "You're a selfish, heartless jackass, Patrick Kavanagh...and an emotionally stunted shell of a man. I don't ever want to see you again...not even if your face is on a Wanted poster. Go to hell."

# Seventeen

$P$atrick had known it was going to be bad…but not that it would hurt so damned much. He unlocked the doors and watched Libby exit his car and his life in one fell swoop. His throat tight, he lowered the window and called her name urgently. "Libby!"

She never hesitated…never turned around.

Patrick struggled through the next several days as if the hours were quicksand threatening to pull him under. Though he found a replacement for Charlise—a male grad student in desperate need of extra cash who was willing to work for five months and then go back to chipping away at the course work for his degree—Patrick felt no sense of relief.

He went through the motions of preparing for his first outdoor adventure group, but the tasks that normally energized and excited him felt burdensome.

Even worse, he was forced to hide out from his family.

He knew his mother well. She had surely put two and two together by now. As Libby's champion, she would have his hide for hurting her.

Even a scheduled trip to LA, a city he normally enjoyed, was torture. All he could see in his mind's eye was Libby sitting at the conference table in her stylish black dress, handing out advice to skittish executives.

Far worse were the two nights he spent in a California hotel, flipping channels when he couldn't sleep. Libby was everywhere. In the big king-size bed, the marble tiled shower, the love seat that was a close twin to a certain settee in New York.

As much as he wanted to avoid facing the music in Silver Glen, he quickly wrapped up his assignment and headed home. His mother's birthday was in two days. Zoe and Cassidy were coordinating a huge bash in the ballroom of Silver Beeches. Though Liam and Maeve had run the lodge together for years, Maeve had finally decided to step down and devote herself to her rapidly expanding crop of grandchildren.

There was no possible way for Patrick to miss such an event. Nor did he want to. But it went without saying that Libby would be in attendance, as well. Even thinking about the possibility of seeing her again made him hard. He hadn't slept worth a damn since she ran from his car.

He relived that moment time after time. In every way he spun the conversation, the truth was, Libby was probably right. But even if he had it all to do over again, he didn't think he could change. The prospect of loving her was too scary.

What if he let himself love her and something happened to her? He had watched Dylan come apart at the seams. Fortunately, Mia was on her way to a complete recovery, but even so, Dylan was probably hovering over her, making sure she obeyed doctor's orders.

Patrick was following the only possible path. He had to keep his distance. He wouldn't let love destroy him.

At last, he came up with what he decided was a rational, well-thought-out plan. He would go to the Silver Dollar—surely Libby had finished moving in by now. And she wouldn't have left town yet—not without taking a few weeks to make some plans about her future and to look for a place to live in New York. He would track Libby down in her upstairs apartment over the saloon and discuss how they would comport themselves during Maeve's celebration.

His heart beat faster at the thought of seeing her again. She wouldn't be able to call him out on the validity of his visit. Neither one of them wanted to hurt or embarrass Maeve.

To mitigate his nervousness and postpone the inevitable, he stopped downstairs in the bar first. It was midafternoon on a Friday. Only a handful of customers lingered after what would have been a predictable lunch-hour rush.

Dylan was behind the bar doing something with the cash drawer. He looked up when Patrick approached. "Howdy, stranger. I thought you'd left town. Nobody's seen or heard from you all week."

"Been busy." He sat down on a leather-topped stool.

Dylan poured him a beer. "You want to go in with Mia and me for Mom's birthday gift? We were thinking about getting her a three-day visit to that new spa over in Asheville…with the works. It's not something she would buy for herself."

"Sounds good. Just tell me how much I owe you." He drained half of his beer and felt his chest tighten. "Do you happen to know if Libby is upstairs at the moment?"

Dylan frowned. "What do you mean?"

"Well, she lives here now, doesn't she? I thought you might keep track of her comings and goings."

Dylan wiped his hands on a clean bar towel, his expression troubled. "She's not living upstairs, man."

"But she was planning to move her stuff here from the hotel. She told me."

"Libby stayed for one night. Then she went back to New York."

Patrick made some excuse to his brother and departed, scraped raw by the look of sympathy on Dylan's face. Patrick felt hollow inside. Life had kicked the heart out of him, and it was his own fault. He hadn't really thought Libby would leave. Granted, he'd told her to go back to New York, but he'd assumed Maeve had helped her get a more suitable job here in Silver Glen while Libby decided if a return to the big city was the right thing to do.

Why would she go back to New York and the friends who had shunned her after her father's arrest?

His stomach curled as he imagined innocent, open-hearted Libby living in some roach-infested apartment in a bad part of town. Possibly in actual physical danger.

God, what had he done?

He raced home and packed a bag. Then he lay awake almost all night to make absolutely sure he knew what he had to do. This was his mess. He was going to make it right. Fortunately, the jet was not in use the next day.

In a moment of absolute clarity, he saw the arrogant blunder he'd made. He'd been so entrenched in the notion that he had no business marrying anyone, he hadn't seen how much he was hurting the one woman who meant the world to him. He loved her. Right or wrong. And he couldn't let her go.

He filed his flight plan and was airborne before 8:00 a.m.

LaGuardia was busy. He had to execute a holding pattern until he was given permission to land. By the time he made it into the city, it was almost noon. He took care of several errands, then checked into the Carlyle and left on foot to walk to Libby's old building.

His idea was far-fetched, but it was the only hope he had of finding her. Fortunately, the doorman was the same old guy Libby had hugged with such fierce affection.

The man recognized Patrick right away. Patrick's plan called for bold-faced confidence.

Patrick smiled. "Hello, there. I'm hoping you can help me. I've come to see Libby and surprise her at her new place, but somehow I lost the address she gave me. Do you perhaps remember what it is? I know the two of you are close."

The elderly gentleman stared at Patrick for the longest time, leaving no doubt that he saw through Patrick's lie. But at last, he relented. He reached in his pocket and took out a scrap of paper. "Don't make me regret this."

Patrick jotted down the information in the note app on his phone and sighed in relief. At least he knew where to start. "Thank you," he said. "I appreciate your help." He pulled a folder from his pocket and handed it to Clarence. "This is an open-ended reservation at my family's hotel. For a two-week stay. You've meant a lot to Libby, and she wanted you to have this."

Hopefully, the tiny white lie would buy him goodwill in both directions.

Clarence smiled broadly. "Tell Miss Libby thank you. And I'll talk to her soon. This is mighty nice. Mighty nice."

Unfortunately, the new apartment was not in walking distance. Patrick was forced to grab a cab and slowly make his way downtown in rush-hour traffic. Contrary to his worst fears, the address pointed him toward TriBeCa... and a trendy collection of redesigned lofts.

This was far beyond anything Libby could afford right now. Had she found a man...an old friend willing to take her in? His gut cramped at the possibility. He took the elevator and rang the bell for 2B. Moments later, he heard footsteps. But nothing happened. There was a security peephole in the door.

Taking a chance, he stared straight at it. "Open up, Libby. I know you're in there, and I'm prepared to stand out here all night."

Libby leaned her forehead against the door and fought back tears. To peek outside and see Patrick in the flesh decimated her hard-won composure. She'd thought she had herself under control.

Turned out, she was wrong.

She cracked the door open, but left the chain on. "Why are you here?" she asked, her tone carefully dispassionate. Obviously it wasn't to declare his undying love for her.

"Maeve's birthday party is tomorrow night. Are you planning to be there?"

The hand behind the door, the one he couldn't see, clenched in a fist. "No. It's too expensive to fly and I don't have a car."

"You're willing to disappoint your mother's good friend…the woman who has done so much for you?"

She was getting tired of trying to read his mood through the crack. But she knew him well enough not to let him in. "Maeve will understand. She knows my financial situation."

"I brought the jet to pick you up, so money is not really an issue."

"I said I'm not going. Goodbye, Patrick."

He stuck his large leather shoe in the opening, foiling her attempt to shut him out. "Now who's being selfish and emotionally stunted?"

Had her words actually wounded him? Why else would he remember them almost verbatim? What would it take to make him leave her alone? And more importantly, what would it take to convince herself she hadn't fallen in love with him?

"What do you want?" she asked. Her heart was in shreds, and she didn't have the will to fight. The past few days had almost done her in. She wanted the man on the other side of the door with every fiber of her being. But she wasn't going to beg. Her dignity was all she had left.

"Please let me in, Libby."

She glanced behind her at the clock on the wall. Spencer would be home soon. This awkward confrontation couldn't last too long. "Fine," she said. "But only for a moment. I have things to do."

After disengaging the chain, she stepped back and let him come in. The dimensions of the loft were generous, but Patrick's size and personality made an impact, even so.

"Have you eaten?" he asked.

"Yes, sorry." But she wasn't sorry at all. And she wasn't going to offer to cook for him.

"This is quite some place."

"Yes. It's very nice."

"I thought all your friends dropped you when your dad went to prison."

"Spencer was doing an eighteen-month stint with the Peace Corps in Bangladesh. Manhattan society news travels slowly over there."

"And now Spencer is back and took you in?"

"Yes."

"And your future employment?"

"Zoe loaned me some money. I interviewed today for a position as a personal shopper at Bergdorf Goodman. Turns out I have skills in that area. As soon as I'm able, I'll be paying her back…"

"And Spencer, too?"

"Of course."

Patrick's expression was moody, as if he resented the fact that she had landed on her feet. What was it to him? He hadn't been willing to give her a job or a place to live... or even a tiny piece of his heart.

"Shall I tell Maeve that I flew up here to get you, but you were too busy to come to her birthday party?" He leaned against the wall in the foyer, his hands shoved in his pockets.

"Why would you do that?"

"To get my way."

Wow. There it was. Not even dressed up.

At that moment, the door opened without ceremony and a large, handsome blond man entered. He stopped short when he saw Patrick. Then he lifted an eyebrow. "Libby?"

"Patrick was just leaving," she said hurriedly. She took the newcomer by the arm and dragged him toward the kitchen, but he refused to go very far. Instead, she had to whisper in his ear.

He straightened after a moment and eyed Patrick with distrust. "I see."

She squeezed his arm. "I'm going back to Silver Glen for a couple of nights. But don't worry about me. I'll be fine."

"You'd better be."

Ten feet away, Patrick practically vibrated with incensed testosterone overload. She had to get him out of the apartment. "You win, Patrick," she said. "But I need some time. I'll meet you at the airport in two hours. Take it or leave it."

He nodded once, scowled at her and walked out.

The blond man chuckled. "Poor bastard. He's madly in love with you and you let him think you're living with me."

"Well, I am living with you," Libby said, giving him a big hug.

"Yeah, but with me *and* Spencer, who happens to be my beautiful, sexy wife."

Libby winced. "I might possibly have led him to believe that Spencer is male…and that *you* are Spencer."

"That's stone-cold, love. But he probably deserved it."

Libby threw some things in a bag, her heart racing with adrenaline. She didn't have a gift for Maeve, but Maeve would understand. Coat, keys, phone, small suitcase. In forty-five minutes, she was running downstairs and out to the street.

Then she stopped dead, because leaning against a lamp-post was Patrick Kavanagh. "I said I would meet you at the airport," she protested.

He shrugged. "I didn't trust you not to run."

There was accusation in his voice…and something else. Fatigue? Sadness? What did he want from her?

"Well, I'm here."

They faced each other silently. Being this close to him ripped apart the web of lies she had told herself to keep going every day. The truth punched her with a ferocity that took her breath. She was madly, deeply, unfortunately in love with Patrick Kavanagh.

He raked a hand through his hair, for the first time revealing a trace of vulnerability. "The airport is shut down for fog. We can't leave until tomorrow morning."

She swallowed. "Okay. Call me and let me know what time." She turned to go back inside the building.

Patrick caught her in two steps, his hands warm on her shoulders. "We need to talk, Libby. Come back to the hotel with me. We'll have dinner there. Casual. Nothing fancy. I'll get you a room if you want it. Or—" He stopped short as if he hadn't meant to say that.

"Or what?"

"Nothing," he muttered. "Never mind. Come have dinner with me. Please."

He was the last person on earth she wanted to have dinner with. And the only person. He didn't deserve to be given the time of day. But she let herself be persuaded. And not because she was weak, and he smelled wonderful. She would hear him out, for Maeve.

After that, Patrick was a complete gentleman. He kept his distance in the cab. At the hotel, he handed her bag to a bellman and steered Libby toward the dining room. The restaurant was conservatively old-school, reminding her of birthday dinners with her parents.

She ordered the lobster bisque. Her appetite lately had been almost nonexistent, but the rich, warm soup was perfect. Patrick chose the duck. Because the captain and servers were attentive, it was easy to let conversation touch on innocuous topics.

But at last, over cappuccino and crème brûlée, Patrick made an overture she hadn't expected. "We need some privacy, Libby. Will you come upstairs with me?"

What did he mean, *privacy*?

Well, hell. She wasn't going to be a coward about this. "For talking? Or something else?"

His throat flushed dark red and his eyes flashed with some strong emotion. "I'll let you make that call."

When he stared at her with storms in his blue-gray irises, she was helpless to resist. Or maybe that was the lie she told herself, because she didn't *want* to resist.

She folded her napkin and set it on the table. "Fine. We'll go upstairs."

The tension in the elevator would have been unbearable except for the older couple who joined them during the brief ride to an upper floor.

At Patrick's door, Libby waited nervously for him to fish the key from his pocket. It was a different room, of course. But the furnishings were similar enough to remind her of every last thing she and Patrick had shared just days earlier in this same city…this same hotel.

Libby took a seat. Patrick stood and paced.

"If you're feeling guilty, I absolve you," she said, the words flat. "You were right. The job at Silver Reflections wasn't suited for me. But you needn't worry. I've landed on my feet, and things are going very well. I should thank you for firing me."

"I didn't exactly *fire* you," he protested, the muscles in his neck corded and tight.

"What would *you* call it?"

He exhaled. "A mistake. A bad mistake. I acted like a complete ass, and I hope you will find it in your heart to forgive me."

"I make no promises. What about the sex?" she asked recklessly, fighting for her happiness, unwilling to let a blindly stubborn man ruin what they had.

"I can't deny it was incredible. But my life was rocking along pretty damn well until you came along." His voice faltered.

"Well, mine wasn't. A thousand apologies, emperor." She made her tone as snide and nasty as she could manage. And she leaped to her feet, no longer content to sit and let him scowl at her.

He grabbed her wrist to reel her in, his chest heaving. "I will not fail at marriage again, Libby."

# Eighteen

Her heart dropped to her feet until she looked deeply into his eyes and saw the secret he was trying so hard to keep. Her jaw dropped. "You love me…"

"No I don't." His denial was automatic but totally unconvincing.

She cupped his face in her hands. "I love you, too, Patrick. But we don't have to get married," she said softly, "if that's what scares you. We can live in sin. You'll be the black sheep of the family."

At last the line between his eyebrows disappeared. "It's the twenty-first century. You'll have to do more than that to get me ostracized."

"I'll try my best. But it will have to be something really awful, won't it? Like maybe you and I making a baby without a ring on my finger? Your mom would hate that."

She saw the muscles in his throat work. "I'd hate it, too," he muttered. "This isn't how things should be, Libby. I've already stood before a priest and repeated marriage vows.

You deserve a man who can come to you with a clean past, a blank slate."

Going against all her instincts, she released him and put the width of the room between them. Still, she couldn't sit down. Too much adrenaline pumped through her veins. She busied herself at the minibar. "Would you like something to drink?"

"No. Look at me, Libby. You know I'm right. You're young and sweet and you deserve all the traditional trappings of an extraordinary wedding. You deserve to be the perfect bride."

She set down the small unopened bottle of liquor. "Here's the truth, Patrick...the last year has taught me that life is seldom perfect. I won't have my father to walk me down the aisle, because he's in prison. My mother won't be at my side helping me pick out a dress, because she took a bottle of pills."

"I'm sorry about all those things."

There was one more secret she knew she should disclose. Something that might make him understand. "Patrick?" She forced herself to perch on the sofa. The gas logs in the fireplace burned cheerfully. "Please sit with me. I want to tell you a story."

His expression guarded, and with reluctance in every line of his body, he nodded. But instead of joining her, he took a chair opposite, putting a low antique table between them as a barrier. "I'm listening."

This was harder than she had thought it would be. But if she didn't tell Patrick, perhaps she would never be free. "You keep calling me innocent, but you had to realize that I wasn't a virgin when you and I made love."

"I knew that. But neither was I. I've never approved of the double standard for women. I don't care about the men in your past, Libby. It's not important."

She leaned forward, her hot face in her hands. Shame flooded her stomach. "Well, it sort of is," she muttered.

Patrick made some kind of motion. "I don't want to hear your confession."

She sat up and stared at him before looking away and shaking her head. "I'm not giving you a choice. I was a very rebellious teenager, Patrick. I'd been spoiled and pampered, and I thought the world was my oyster. I'd barely dated at all, because my parents were so strict."

Patrick inhaled sharply. "Libby…"

"Don't interrupt. Please. The thing is, my father's best friend was newly divorced that year. He began flirting with me every time he came over to the apartment. I didn't really think of it as flirting. But I was smug about the fact that an older, sophisticated man was interested in my thoughts and opinions. It made me feel very grown-up."

Beneath his breath, Patrick said a word that was succinct and vehement. She had to ignore him to get through this.

"I turned sixteen in February. That fall was the beginning of my senior year. Most of my classmates had boyfriends, but I didn't. So I started telling everyone about *Mitch*."

"Was that his real name?"

She shrugged. "His middle name. I wasn't entirely stupid. I didn't want to get him or me in trouble. But as time passed and no one ever saw my 'boyfriend' at parties or other social occasions, they began to accuse me of making him up. The more teasing I took at school, the closer I grew to my father's friend. The attention of this handsome, very masculine man soothed my adolescent feelings of inadequacy."

"A man old enough to be your father."

"It didn't seem that way. To me, he was close to perfect."

"So what happened?"

Apparently, in spite of himself, Patrick wanted to know.

"In October, my father had to go to a financial seminar in Chicago. He wanted my mother and me to accompany him. But the trip sounded beyond boring to a teenage girl, even though my mom promised me shopping. I insisted that I was almost an adult and that they could certainly trust me. I begged them to let me stay home for the two nights they would be away."

"Oh, Libby…"

"It wasn't really a big deal. I planned to watch *inappropriate* movies on cable and paint my toenails and text with my friends. Maybe even sneak into my parents' liquor cabinet and have a single glass of sherry. I felt very daring and independent."

"And then Mitch came over."

"How did you know that?"

"It's not that hard to figure out. He knew you were going to be alone."

Libby grimaced. "I was an easy mark. He pretended he dropped by to see Daddy, and then feigned surprise that my father wasn't home. Later on, of course, I understood that Mitch knew exactly where my parents were and that I hadn't gone with them to Chicago. But at the time, it seemed like a happy accident. I asked him to come in."

Patrick had gone white beneath his tan. "He raped you."

Even now, the memory of that night made her shudder. "I wish it were that simple. I didn't understand all that much about men. I certainly didn't know that when they started drinking they were more dangerous. But I was having so much fun and he was complimenting me on my looks and my intelligence…anyway, when he kissed me the first time, I thought it was okay. For a minute."

"And afterward?"

"Something inside me said I should go to my bedroom

and lock my door. But I didn't want him to think of me as a child. So I ignored that little voice. And I paid the price."

"God, Libby…"

Tears stung her eyes, though she didn't let them fall. "It was a long time ago. And I'm fine…really I am. I just wanted you to know that I wouldn't come to marriage unscathed, either. Not that you've asked me, but you know…"

Patrick staggered to his feet, his heart and his composure shattering into pieces like brittle glass. He went to the sofa and sat down, scooping her into his lap. For a long time, they just sat there…not speaking, her head tucked against his shoulder.

He stroked her fiery hair, wanting desperately to find the son of a bitch with the middle name Mitch and avenge Libby's honor.

At last, he drew a deep breath and let go of the past that had held him with invisible chains. "I adore you, Libby Parkhurst. How could I not? You're beautiful and brave and you have the most extraordinary outlook on life." He tipped her backward over his arm and kissed her, shuddering with relief as she kissed him in return.

When they separated and sat side by side, her green eyes were damp, but then his were, too, so they were even. "Don't move," he said.

Her face expressed first puzzlement and then astonishment when he slid off the sofa and onto one knee, pushing the table aside. Reaching into his pocket, he pulled out a turquoise leather box and flipped it open. "Marry me, Libby," he pleaded, the words hoarse, his throat raw.

She stared at the multicarat single stone as if it were a snake. "You have a ring?"

Her bewilderment made him feel lower than low. "Of course, I do," he said. "I'll change this for a diamond if you want, but I've always thought redheads should wear emeralds." Libby didn't protest when he slid the simple platinum band with the exotic jewel onto her finger.

She held her hand up, her eyes wide. "It's extraordinary."

"I have no doubts about us, Libby, not anymore. And it's not because of your confession. You've opened my eyes to how stupid I've been to deliberately throw away something so amazingly good. I'm sorry I insulted you and fired you and tried to break your heart. I was an idiot. I bought the ring this afternoon, but then I got cold feet." He rested his forehead against her knee. He'd said his piece. The outcome was up to her now.

Her silence lasted too damn long. When he felt her fingers in his hair, he braced for a refusal.

But Libby took him by surprise. She slid down beside him, her legs curled to one side. "This is a very beautiful rug," she said. "I suppose we shouldn't do anything to ruin it."

He scowled at her. "Damn it, Libby. Don't toy with me. I've had a hell of a day."

"And whose fault is that?"

"I know I said I didn't care about other men in your life, and I really don't, but tell me one thing. Is Spencer expecting to share your bed? He's a big guy, and I want to know if I'm going to have to fight for your hand."

Libby's eyes widened, and she laughed, staring down at her fingers as if mesmerized by the brilliant green stone Patrick had spent several hours choosing. "Spencer is my dear friend. She and I were best buddies in school. The man you met at the loft is her husband, Derek."

Patrick exhaled, torn between frustration at Libby's deliberate deception and relief that no one else had a claim on his fiancée. "You're going to lead me in a merry dance, aren't you? I'll never be able to turn my back. And when you gang up with my sisters-in-law, Lord help us all."

He stretched out his legs and banged his shin on the table leg. "Wait a minute," he said, aggrieved. "You haven't said you'll marry me."

"I didn't?" Guileless green eyes looked up at him.

He started to sweat. "Say it, Libby. Right now."

She sighed, leaning forward to unbutton his shirt. "Yes, Patrick Kavanagh. I will marry you. Now, are you satisfied?"

He kissed her hard, moving over her and pressing her into the sofa. But it was a damned uncomfortable position. "I'm not satisfied at all," he stuttered. "Bedroom. Now." He dragged her to her feet, trying to undress her and walk at the same time. They made it as far as the still-closed door, but his patience frayed.

He lifted her hands over her head, trapping her against the polished wood with the weight of his body. Her breasts, mostly exposed in a sexy bra, heaved.

Libby's gaze was dreamy. "Let's come here for our honeymoon," she said.

"But during the summer. When you don't have to wear so many clothes." He gave up on the wrist-holding thing and unzipped her pants. "Help me, woman."

Finally, aeons later, they were both nude. He held her tightly, his face buried in her hair. "This is forever. I hope you know that."

Libby sighed deeply. "I'm counting on it, my love."

Twenty-four hours later, Libby stood in one of the private salons at the Silver Beeches Lodge and hid a yawn behind her hand. The emerald ring hung on a chain tucked inside her dress. All around her, the Kavanagh family, along with an intimate circle of friends, laughed and danced and partied. Maeve, the guest of honor, beamed continuously, delighted to have all her loved ones under one roof.

By prior agreement, Patrick and Libby had arrived at the festivities separately. For the past two hours they had stayed on opposite sides of the room. Either Dylan or Zoe must have warned everyone not to make a big deal about Libby's presence after a weeklong absence, because no one said a word out of place. All the attention was centered on Maeve—as it should be.

Still, it was a good bet that all the Kavanaghs knew Libby was no longer working for Patrick, and that things had ended badly.

After a sumptuous dinner, Maeve opened gifts. Her family and friends showered her with offerings of love and affection. For a brief moment, Libby allowed herself to grieve the fact that her own children would have only one grandmother. But then the moment passed.

She was luckier than most.

At last, when the babies were asleep and even the grown-ups were starting to fade, it was clear the party was over. Patrick stepped to the center of the room and gave his mother a hug. "I have one last gift for you, Mom."

Maeve seemed confused. "But I thought the spa thing had your name on it, too."

Little by little, the room fell silent. All eyes were on Patrick. "This is something more personal," he said.

Unobtrusively, Libby removed the emerald from its resting place and slipped it onto her left finger. It had pained her not to wear it, even for this one brief evening.

Patrick stood—tall and strong—with an almost palpable air of contentment and joy surrounding him.

Maeve stared at her boy, her brow creased. "Well, don't keep me in suspense. Where is it?"

Patrick grinned broadly, crooking a finger. "It's not an *it*. It's a *who*."

Libby threaded her way through the crowd, smiling as

the swell of exclamations followed her progress. When she joined Patrick, he put an arm around her.

"Mom," he said. "I'd like to present my fiancée, Libby Parkhurst, soon to be the daughter of your heart."

Maeve burst into tears, and the entire room fairly exploded with excitement. Libby lost track of the hugs and kisses and well wishes.

When some of the furor finally died down, Maeve held her close and whispered in her ear. "Thank you, Libby. Look at him. He's beaming."

And indeed he was. Libby's heart turned over. If she had harbored any last doubts, seeing Patrick like this in the bosom of his family and so obviously exultant and happy made her own heart swell with emotion.

Patrick finally reclaimed his fiancée and dragged her out to the car. He leaned her against the hood and kissed her long and slow. "Come home with me, my love."

Libby wrapped her arms around his neck, feeling the beat of his heart against hers. "I thought you'd never ask…"

\* \* \* \* \*

# NEVER TOO LATE
## Brenda Jackson

# *Chapter 1*

Twelve days and counting...

Pushing a lock of twisted hair that had fallen in her face behind her ear, Sienna Bradford, soon to become Sienna Davis once again, straightened her shoulders as she walked into the cabin she'd once shared with her husband—soon-to-be ex-husband.

She glanced around. Had it been just three years ago when Dane had brought her here for the first time? Three years ago when the two of them had sat there in front of the fireplace after making love, and planned their wedding? Promising that no matter what, their marriage would last forever? She took a deep breath knowing that for them, forever would end in twelve days in Judge Ratcliff's chambers.

Just thinking about it made her heart ache, but she decided it wouldn't help matters to have a pity party. What was done was done and things just hadn't worked out between her and Dane like they'd hoped. There was nothing to do now but move on with her life. But first, according to a letter her attorney had received from Dane's attorney a few days ago, she had ten days to clear out any and all of her belongings from the cabin, and the sooner she got the task done, the better. Dane had agreed to let her keep the condo if she returned full ownership of the cabin to him. She'd had no problem with that, since he had owned it before they married.

Sienna crossed the room, shaking off the March chill. According to forecasters, a snowstorm was headed toward the Smoky Mountains within the next seventy-two hours, which meant she had to hurry and pack up her stuff and take the two-hour drive back to Charlotte. Once she got home she intended to stay inside and curl up in bed with a good book. Sienna smiled, thinking that a "do nothing" weekend was just what she needed in her too frantic life.

Her smile faded when she considered that since starting her own interior decorating business a year and a half ago, she'd been extremely busy—and she had to admit that was when her marital problems with Dane had begun.

Sienna took a couple of steps toward the bedroom to begin packing her belongings when she heard the sound of the door opening. Turning quickly, she suddenly remembered she had forgotten to lock the door. Not smart when she was alone in a secluded cabin high up in the mountains, and a long way from civilization.

A scream quickly died in her throat when the person who walked in—standing a little over six feet with dark eyes, close-cropped black hair, chestnut coloring and a medium build—was none other than her soon-to-be ex.

From the glare on his face, she could tell he wasn't happy to see her. But so what? She wasn't happy to see him, either, and couldn't help wondering why he was there.

Before she could swallow the lump in her throat to ask, he crossed his arms over his broad chest, intensified his glare and said in that too sexy voice she knew so well, "I thought that was your car parked outside, Sienna. What are you doing here?"

# Chapter 2

Dane wet his suddenly dry lips and immediately decided he needed a beer. Lucky for him there was a six-pack in the refrigerator from the last time he'd come to the cabin. But he didn't intend on moving an inch until Sienna told him what she was doing there.

She was nervous, he could tell. Well, that was too friggin bad. She was the one who'd filed for the divorce—he hadn't. But since she had made it clear that she wanted him out of her life, he had no problem giving her what she wanted, even if the pain was practically killing him. But she'd never know that.

"What do you think I'm doing here?" she asked smartly, reclaiming his absolute attention.

"If I knew, I wouldn't have asked," he said, giving her the same unblinking stare. And to think that at one time he actually thought she was his whole world. At some point during their marriage she had changed and transitioned into quite a character—someone he was certain he didn't know anymore.

She met his gaze for a long, level moment before placing her hands on her hips. Doing so drew his attention to her body; a body he'd seen naked countless times, a body he knew as well as his own; a body he used to ease into during the heat of passion to receive pleasure so keen and satisfying, just thinking about it made him hard.

"The reason I'm here, Dane Bradford, is because your attorney sent mine this nasty little letter demanding that I remove my stuff within ten days, and this weekend was better than next weekend. However, no thanks to you, I still had to close the shop early to beat traffic and the bad weather."

He actually smiled at the thought of her having to do that. "And I bet it almost killed you to close your shop early. Heaven forbid. You probably had to cancel a couple of appointments. Something I could never get you to do for me."

Sienna rolled her eyes. They'd had this same argument over and over again and it all boiled down to the same thing. He thought her job meant more to her than he did because of all the time she'd put into it. But what really irked her with that accusation was that before she'd even entertained the idea of quitting her job and embarking on her own business, they had talked about it and what it would mean. She would have to work her butt off and network to build a new clientele; and then there would be time spent working on decorating proposals, spending long hours in many beautiful homes of the rich and famous. And he had understood and had been supportive… at least in the beginning.

But then he began complaining that she was spending too much time away from home, away from him. Things only got worse from there, and now she was a woman who had gotten married at twenty-four and was getting divorced at twenty-seven.

"Look, Dane, it's too late to look back, reflect and complain. In twelve days you'll be free of me and I'll be free of you. I'm sure there's a woman out there who has the time and patience to—"

"Now, that's a word you don't know the meaning of, Sienna," Dane interrupted. "*Patience.* You were always in a rush, and your tolerance level for the least little thing was zero. Yeah, I know I probably annoyed the hell out of you at times. But then there were times you annoyed me, as well. Neither of us is perfect."

Sienna let out a deep breath. "I never said I was perfect, Dane."

"No, but you sure as hell acted like you thought you were, didn't you?"

# Chapter 3

Dane's question struck a nerve. Considering her background, how could he assume Sienna thought she was perfect? She had come from a dysfunctional family if ever there was one. Her mother hadn't loved her father, her father loved all women except her mother, and neither seemed to love their only child. Sienna had always combated lack of love with doing the right thing, thinking that if she did, her parents would eventually love her. It didn't work. But still, she had gone through high school and college being the good girl, thinking being good would eventually pay off and earn her the love she'd always craved.

In her mind, it had when she'd met Dane, the man least likely to fall in love with her. He was the son of the millionaire Bradfords who'd made money in land development. She hadn't been his family's choice and they made sure she knew it every chance they got. Whenever she was around them, they made her feel inadequate, like she didn't measure up to their society friends, and since she didn't come from a family with a prestigious background, she wasn't good enough for their son.

She bet they wished they'd never hired the company she'd been working for to decorate their home. That's how she and Dane had met. She'd been going over fabric swatches with his mother and he'd walked in after playing a game of tennis. The rest was history. But the question of the hour was: Had she been so busy trying to succeed the past year and a half, trying to be the perfect business owner, that she eventually alienated the one person who'd mattered most to her?

"Can't answer that. Can you?" Dane said, breaking into her thoughts. "Maybe that will give you something to think about twelve days from now when you put your John Hancock on the divorce papers. Now if you'll excuse me, I have something to do," he said, walking around her toward the bedroom.

"Wait. You never said why *you're* here!"

He stopped. The intensity of his gaze sent shivers of heat through her entire body. And it didn't help matters that he was wearing jeans and a dark brown leather bomber jacket that made him look sexy as hell…as usual. "I was here a couple of weekends ago and left something behind. I came to get it."

"Were you alone?" The words rushed out before she could hold them back and immediately she wanted to smack herself. The last thing she wanted was for him to think she cared…even if she did.

He hooked his thumbs in his jeans and continued to hold her gaze. "Would it matter to you if I weren't?"

She couldn't look at him, certain he would see her lie when she replied, "No, it wouldn't matter. What you do is none of my business."

"That's what I thought." And then he walked off toward the bedroom and closed the door.

Sienna frowned. That was another thing she didn't like about Dane. He never stayed around to finish one of their arguments. Thanks to her parents she was a pro at it, but Dane would always walk away after giving some smart parting remark that only made her that much more angry. He didn't know how to fight fair. He didn't know how to fight at all. He'd come from a family too dignified for such nonsense.

Moving toward the kitchen to see if there was anything of hers in there, Sienna happened to glance out the window.

"Oh, my God," she said, rushing over to the window. It was snowing already. No, it wasn't just snowing… There was a full-scale blizzard going on outside. What happened to the seventy-two-hour warning?

She heard Dane when he came out of the bedroom. He looked beyond her and out the window, uttering one hell of a curse word before quickly walking to the door, slinging it open and stepping outside.

In just that short period of time, everything was beginning to turn white. The last time they'd had a sudden snowstorm such as this had been a few years ago. It had been so bad the media had nicknamed it the "Beast from the East."

It seemed the Beast was back and it had turned downright spiteful. Not only was it acting ugly outside, it had placed Sienna in one hell of a predicament. She was stranded in a cabin in the Smoky Mountains with her soon-to-be ex. Things couldn't get any more bizarre than that.

# *Chapter 4*

Moments later, when Dane stepped back into the cabin, slamming the door behind him, Sienna could tell he was so mad he could barely breathe.

"What's wrong, Dane? You being forced to cancel a date tonight?" she asked snidely. A part of her was still upset at the thought that he might have brought someone here a couple of weekends ago when they weren't officially divorced yet. The mere fact they had been separated for six months didn't count. She hadn't gone out with anyone. Indulging in a relationship with another man hadn't even crossed her mind.

He took a step toward her and she refused to back up. She was determined to maintain her ground and her composure, although the intense look in his eyes was causing crazy things to happen to her body, like it normally did whenever they were alone for any period of time. There may have been a number of things wrong with their marriage, but lack of sexual chemistry had never been one of them.

"Do you know what this means?" he asked, his voice shaking in anger.

She tilted her head to one side. "Other than I'm being forced to remain here with you for a couple of hours, no, I don't know what it means."

She saw his hands ball into fists at his sides and knew he was probably fighting the urge to strangle her. "We're not talking about hours, Sienna. Try days. Haven't you been listening to the weather reports?"

She glared at him. "Haven't you? I'm not here by myself."

"Yes, but I thought I could come up here and in ten minutes max get what I came for, and leave before the bad weather kicked in."

Sienna regretted that she hadn't been listening to the weather reports, at least not in detail. She'd known that a snowstorm was headed toward the mountains within seventy-two hours, which was why she'd thought, like Dane, that she had time to rush and get in and out before the nasty weather hit. Anything other than that, she was clueless. And what was he saying about them being up here for days instead of hours? "Yes, I did listen to the weather reports, but evidently I missed something."

He shook his head. "Evidently you missed a lot, if you think this storm is going to blow over in a couple of hours. According to forecasters, what you see isn't the worst of it, and because of that unusual cold front hovering about in the east, it may last for days."

She swallowed deeply. The thought of spending *days* alone in a cabin with Dane didn't sit well with her. "How many days are we talking about?"

"Try three or four."

She didn't want to try any at all, and as she continued to gaze into his eyes she saw a look of worry replace the anger in their dark depths. Then she knew what had him upset.

"Do we have enough food and supplies up here to hold us for three or four days?" she asked, as she began to nervously gnaw on her lower lip. The magnitude of the situation they were in was slowly dawning on her, and when he didn't answer immediately she knew they were in trouble.

*Chapter 5*

Dane saw the panic that suddenly lined Sienna's face. He wished he could say he didn't give a damn, but there was no way that he could. This woman would always matter to him whether she was married to him or not. From the moment he had walked into his father's study that day and their gazes had connected, he had known then, as miraculous at it had seemed, and without a word spoken between them, that he was meant to love her. And for a while he had convinced her of that, but not anymore. Evidently, at some point during their marriage, she began believing otherwise.

"Dane?"

He rubbed his hand down his face, trying to get his thoughts together. Given the situation they were in, he knew honesty was foremost. But then he'd always been honest with her, however, he doubted she could say the same for herself. "To answer your question, Sienna, I'm not sure. Usually I keep the place well stocked of everything, but like I said earlier, I was here a couple of weekends ago, and I used a lot of the supplies then."

He refused to tell her that in a way it had been her fault.

Receiving those divorce papers had driven him here, to wallow in self-pity, vent out his anger and drink his pain away with a bottle of Johnny Walker Red. "I guess we need to go check things out," he said, trying not to get as worried as she was beginning to look.

He followed her into the kitchen, trying not to watch the sway of her hips as she walked in front of him. The hot, familiar sight of her in a pair of jeans and pullover sweater had him cursing under his breath and summoning up a quick remedy for the situation he found himself in. The thought of being stranded for any amount of time with Sienna wasn't good.

He stopped walking when she flung open the refrigerator. His six-pack of beer was still there, but little else. But then he wasn't studying the contents of the refrigerator as much as he was studying her. She was bent over, looking inside, but all he could think of was another time he had walked into this kitchen and found her in that same position, and wearing nothing more than his T-shirt that had barely covered her bottom. It hadn't taken much for him to go into a crazed fit of lust and quickly remove his pajama bottoms and take her right then and there, against the refrigerator, giving them both the orgasm of a lifetime.

"Thank goodness there are some eggs in here," she said, intruding on his heated thoughts down memory lane. "About half a dozen. And there's a loaf of bread that looks edible. There's some kind of meat in the freezer, but I'm not sure what it is, though. Looks like chicken."

She turned around and her pouty mouth tempted him to kiss it, devour it and make her moan. He watched her sigh deeply and then she gave him a not-so-hopeful gaze and said, "Our rations don't look good, Dane. What are we going to do?"

# Chapter 6

Sienna's breath caught when the corners of Dane's mouth tilted in an irresistible smile. She'd seen the look before. She knew that smile and she also recognized that bulge pressing against his zipper. She frowned. "Don't even think it, Dane."

He leaned back against the kitchen counter. Hell, he wanted to do more than think it, he wanted to do it. But, of course, he would pretend he hadn't a clue as to what she was talking about. "What?"

Her frown deepened. "And don't act all innocent with me. I know what you were thinking."

A smile tugged deeper at Dane's lips knowing she probably did. There were some things a man couldn't hide and a rock-solid hard-on was one of them. He decided not to waste his time and hers pretending the chemistry between them was dead when they both knew it was still very much alive. "Don't ask me to apologize. It's not my fault you have so much sex appeal and my desire for you is automatic, even when we're headed for divorce court."

Dane saying the word *divorce* was a stark reminder that

their life together, as they once knew it, would be over in twelve days. "Let's get back to important matters, Dane, like our survival. On a positive note, we might be able to make due if we cut back on meals, which may be hard for you with your ferocious appetite."

A wicked sounding chuckle poured from his throat. "Which one?"

Sienna swallowed as her pulse pounded in response to Dane's question. She was quickly reminded, although she wished there was some way she could forget, that her husband…or soon-to-be ex…did have two appetites. One was of a gastric nature and the other purely sexual. Thoughts of the purely sexual one had intense heat radiating all through her. Dane had devoured every inch of her body in ways she didn't even want to think about. Especially now.

She placed her hands on her hips knowing he was baiting her; really doing a hell of a lot more than that. He was stirring up feelings inside her that were making it hard for her to think straight. "Get serious, Dane."

"I am." He then came to stand in front of her. "Did you bring anything with you?"

She lifted a brow. "Anything like what?"

"Stuff to snack on. You're good for that. How you do it without gaining a pound is beyond me."

She shrugged, refusing to tell him that she used to work it off with all those in-bed, out-of-bed exercises they used to do. If he hadn't noticed then she wouldn't tell him that in six months without him in her bed, she had gained five pounds. "I might have a candy bar or two in the car."

He smiled. "That's all?"

She rolled her eyes upward. "Okay, okay, I might have a couple of bags of chips, too." She decided not to mention the three boxes of Girl Scout cookies that had been purchased that morning from a little girl standing in front of a grocery store.

"I hadn't planned to spend the night here, Dane. I had merely thought I could quickly pack things and leave."

He nodded. "Okay, I'll get the snacks from your car while I'm outside checking on some wood we'll need for the fire. The power is still on, but I can't see that lasting too much longer. I wished I would have gotten that generator fixed."

Her eyes widened in alarm. "You didn't?"

"No. So you might want to go around and gather up all the candles you can. And there should be a box of matches in one of these drawers."

"Okay."

Dane turned to leave. He then turned back around. She was nibbling on her bottom lip as he assumed she would be. "And stop worrying. We're going to make it."

When he walked out the room, Sienna leaned back against the closed refrigerator, thinking those were the exact words he'd said to her three years ago when he had asked her to marry him. Now she *was* worried because they didn't have a proved track record.

## Chapter 7

After putting on the snow boots he kept at the cabin, Dane made his way out the doors, grateful for the time he wouldn't be in Sienna's presence. Being around her and still loving her like he did was hard. Even now he didn't know the reason for the divorce, other than what was noted in the papers he'd been served that day a few weeks ago. Irreconcilable differences…whatever the hell that was supposed to mean.

Sienna hadn't come to him so they could talk about any problems they were having. He had come home one day and she had moved out. He still was at a loss as to what could have been so wrong with their marriage that she could no longer see a future for them.

He would always recall that time as being the lowest point in his life. For days it was as if a part of him was missing. It had taken a while to finally pull himself together and realize she wasn't coming back no matter how many times he'd asked her to. And all it took was the receipt of that divorce petition to make him realize that Sienna wanted him out of her life, and actually believed that whatever issues kept them apart couldn't be resolved.

A little while later Dane had gathered more wood to put with the huge stack already on the back porch, glad that at least, if nothing else, they wouldn't freeze to death. The cabin was equipped with enough toiletries to hold them for at least a week, which was a good thing. And he hadn't wanted to break the news to Sienna that the meat in the freezer wasn't chicken, but deer meat that one of his clients had given him a couple of weeks ago after a hunting trip. It was good to eat, but he knew Sienna well enough to know she would have to be starving before she would consume any of it.

After rubbing his icy hands on his jeans, he stuck them into his pockets to keep them from freezing. Walking around the house, he strolled over to her car, opened the door and found the candy bars, chips and… Girl Scout cookies, he noted, lifting a brow. She hadn't mentioned them, and he saw they were her favorite kind, as well as his. He quickly recalled the first year they were married and how they shared the cookies as a midnight snack after making love. He couldn't help but smile as he remembered that night and others where they had spent time together, not just in bed but cooking in the kitchen, going to movies, concerts, parties, having picnics and just plain sitting around and talking for hours.

He suddenly realized that one of the things that had been missing from their marriage for a while was communication. When had they stopped talking? The first thought that grudgingly came to mind was when she'd begun bringing work home, letting it intrude on what had always been their time together. That's when they had begun living in separate worlds.

Dane breathed in deeply. He wanted to get back into Sienna's world and he definitely wanted her back in his.

He didn't want a divorce. He wanted to keep his wife but he refused to resort to any type of manipulating, dominating or controlling tactics to do it. What he and Sienna needed was to use this weekend to keep it honest and talk openly about what had gone wrong with their marriage. They would go further by finding ways to resolve things. He still loved her and wanted to believe that deep down she still loved him.

There was only one way to find out.

## *Chapter 8*

Sienna glanced around the room seeing all the lit candles and thinking just how romantic they made the cabin look. Taking a deep breath, she frowned in irritation, thinking that romance should be the last thing on her mind. Dane was her soon-to-be ex-husband. Whatever they once shared was over, done with, had come to a screeching end.

*If only the memories weren't so strong...*

She glanced out the window and saw him piling wood on the back porch. Never in her wildest dreams would she have thought her day would end up this way, with her and Dane being stranded together at the cabin—a place they always considered as their favorite getaway spot. During the first two years of their marriage, they would come here every chance they got, but in the past year she could recall them coming only once. Somewhere along the way she had stopped allowing them time even for this.

She sighed deeply, recalling how important it had been to her at the beginning of their marriage for them to make time to talk about matters of interest, whether trivial or important. They had always been attuned to each other, and

Dane had always been a good listener, which to her conveyed a sign of caring and respect. But the last couple of times they had tried to talk ended up with them snapping at each other, which only built bitterness and resentment.

The lights blinked and she knew they were about to go out. She was glad that she had taken the initiative to go into the kitchen and scramble up some eggs earlier. And she was inwardly grateful that if she had to get stranded in the cabin during a snowstorm that Dane was here with her. Heaven knows she would have been a basket case had she found herself up here alone.

The lights blinked again before finally going out, but the candles provided the cabin with plenty of light. Not sure if the temperatures outside would cause the pipes to freeze, she had run plenty of water in the bathtub and kitchen sink, and filled every empty jug with water for them to drink. She'd also found batteries to put in the radio so they could keep up with any reports on the weather.

"I saw the lights go out. Are you okay?"

Sienna turned around. Dane was leaning in the doorway with his hands stuck in the pockets of his jeans. The pose made him look incredibly sexy. "Yes, I'm okay. I was able to get the candles all lit and there are plenty more."

"That's good."

"Just in case the pipes freeze and we can't use the shower, I filled the bathtub up with water so we can take a bath that way." At his raised brow she quickly added, "Separately, of course. And I made sure I filled plenty of bottles of drinking water, too."

He nodded. "Sounds like you've been busy."

"So have you. I saw through the window when you put all that wood on the porch. It will probably come in handy."

He moved away from the door. "Yes, and with the electricity out I need to go ahead and get the fire started."

Sienna swallowed as she watched him walk toward her

on his way to the fireplace, and not for the first time she thought about how remarkably handsome he was. He had that certain charisma that made women get hot all over just looking at him.

It suddenly occurred to her that he'd already got a fire started, and the way it was spreading through her was about to make her burst into flames.

# Chapter 9

"You okay?" Dane asked Sienna as he walked toward her with a smile.

She nodded and cleared her throat. "Yes, why do you ask?"

"Because you're looking at me funny."

"Oh." She was vaguely aware of him walking past her to kneel in front of the fireplace. She turned and watched him, saw him move the wood around before taking a match and lighting it to start a fire. He was so good at kindling things, whether wood or the human body.

"If you like, I can make something for dinner," she decided to say, otherwise she would continue to stand there and say nothing while staring at him. It was hard trying to be normal in a rather awkward situation.

"What are our options?" he asked without looking around.

She chuckled. "An egg sandwich and tea. I made both earlier before the power went off."

He turned at that and his gaze caught hers. A smile crinkled his eyes. "Do I have a choice?"

"Not if you want to eat."

"What about those Girl Scout cookies I found in your car?"

Her eyes narrowed. "They're off-limits. You can have one of the candy bars, but the cookies are mine."

His mouth broke into a wide grin. "You have enough cookies to share, so stop being selfish."

He turned back around and she made a face at him behind his back. He was back to stoking the fire and her gaze went to his hands. Those hands used to be the givers of so much pleasure and almost ran neck and neck with his mouth…but not quite. His mouth was in a class by itself. But still, she could recall those same hands, gentle, provoking, moving all over her body; touching her everywhere and doing things to her that mere hands weren't suppose to do. However, she never had any complaints.

"Did you have any plans for tonight, Sienna?"

His words intruded into her heated thoughts. "No, why?"

"Just wondering. You thought I had a date tonight. What about you?"

She shrugged. "No. As far as I'm concerned, until we sign those final papers, I'm still legally married and wouldn't feel right going out with someone."

He turned around and locked his eyes with hers. "I know what you mean," he said. "I wouldn't feel right going out with someone else."

Heat seeped through her every pore with his words. "So you haven't been dating, either?"

"No."

There were a number of questions she wanted to ask him—how he spent his days, his nights, what his family thought of their pending divorce, what he thought of it, was he ready for it to be over for them to go their separate ways—but there was no way she could ask him any of those things. "I guess I'll go put dinner on the table."

He chuckled. "An egg sandwich and tea?"

"Yes." She turned to leave.

"Sienna?"

She turned back around. "Yes?"

"I don't like being stranded, but since I am, I'm glad it's with you."

For a moment she couldn't say anything, then she cleared her throat while backing up a couple of steps. "Ah, yeah right, same here." She backed up some more then said, "I'll go set out the food now." And then she turned and quickly left the room.

# Chapter 10

Sienna glanced up when she heard Dane walk into the kitchen and smiled. "Your feast awaits you."

"Whoopee."

She laughed. "Hey, I know the feeling. I'm glad I had a nice lunch today in celebration. I took on a new client."

Dane came and joined her at the table. "Congratulations."

"Thank you."

She took a bite of her scrambled egg sandwich and a sip of her tea and then said, "It's been a long time since you seemed genuinely pleased with my accomplishments."

He glanced up after taking a sip of his own tea and stared at her for a moment. "I know and I'm sorry about that. It was hard being replaced by your work, Sienna."

She lifted her head and stared at him, met his gaze. She saw the tightness of his jaw and the firm set of his mouth. He actually believed that something could replace him with her and knowing that hit a raw and sensitive nerve. "My work never replaced you, Dane. Why did you begin feeling that way?"

Dane leaned back in his chair, tilted his head slightly. He was more than mildly surprised with her question. It was then he realized that she really didn't know. Hadn't a clue. This was the opportunity that he wanted; what he was hoping they would have. Now was the time to put aside anger, bitterness, foolish pride and whatever else was working at destroying their marriage. Now was the time for complete honesty. "You started missing dinner. Not once but twice, sometimes three times a week. Eventually, you stopped making excuses and didn't show up."

What he'd said was the truth. "But I was working and taking on new clients," she defended. "You said you would understand."

"And I did for a while and up to a point. But there is such a thing as common courtesy and mutual respect, Sienna. In the end I felt like I'd been thrown by the wayside, that you didn't care anymore about us, our love or our marriage."

She narrowed her eyes. "And why didn't you say something?"

"When? I was usually asleep when you got home and when I got up in the morning you were too sleepy to discuss anything. I invited you to lunch several times, but you couldn't fit me into your schedule."

"I had appointments."

"Yes, and I always felt because of it that your clients were more important."

"Still, I wished you would have let me know how you felt," she said, after taking another sip of tea.

"I did, several times. But you weren't listening."

She sighed deeply. "We used to know how to communicate."

"Yes, at one time we did, didn't we?" Dane said quietly. "But I'm also to blame for the failure of our marriage, our lack of communication. And then there were the problems you were having with my parents. When it came to you, I never hesitated letting my parents know when they were out of line and that I wouldn't put up with their treatment of you. But then I felt that at some point you needed to start believing that what they thought didn't matter and stand up to them.

"I honestly thought I was doing the right thing when I decided to just stay out of it and give you the chance to deal with them, to finally put them in their place. Instead, you let them erode away at your security and confidence to the point where you felt you had to prove you were worthy of them…and of me. That's what drove you to be so successful, wasn't it, Sienna? Feeling the need to prove something is what working all those long hours was all about, wasn't it?"

## Chapter 11

Sienna quickly got up from the table and walked to the window. It was turning dark but she could clearly see that things hadn't let up. It was still snowing outside, worse than an hour before. She tried to concentrate on what was beyond that window and not on the question Dane had asked her.

"Sienna?"

Moments later she turned back around to face Dane, knowing he was waiting on her response. "What do you want me to say, Dane? Trust me, you don't want to get me started since you've always known how your family felt about me."

His brow furrowed sharply as he moved from the table to join her at the window, coming to stand directly in front of her. "And you've known it didn't matter one damn iota. Why would you let it continue to matter to you?"

She shook her head, tempted to bare her soul but fighting not to. "But you don't understand how important it was for your family to accept me, to love me."

Dane stepped closer, looked into eyes that were fighting to keep tears at bay.

"Wasn't my love enough, Sienna? I'd told you countless time that you didn't marry my family, you married me. I'm not proud of the fact that my parents think too highly of themselves and our family name at times, but I've constantly told you it didn't matter. Why can't you believe me?"

When she didn't say anything, he sighed deeply. "You've been around people with money before. Do all of them act like my parents?"

She thought of her best friend's family. The Steeles. "No."

"Then what should that tell you? They're my parents. I know that they aren't close to being perfect, but I love them."

"And I never wanted to do anything to make you stop loving them."

He reached up and touched her chin. "And that's what this is about, isn't it? Why you filed for a divorce. You thought that you could."

Sienna angrily wiped at a tear she couldn't contain any longer. "I didn't ever want you to have to choose."

Dane's heart ached. Evidently she didn't know just how much he loved her. "There wouldn't have been a choice to make. You're my wife. I love you. I will always love you. When we married, we became one."

He leaned down and brushed a kiss on her cheek, then several. He wanted to devour her mouth, deepen the kiss and escalate it to a level he needed it to be, but he couldn't. He wouldn't. What they needed was to talk, to communicate to try and fix whatever was wrong with their marriage. He pulled back. It was hard when he heard her soft sigh, her heated moan.

He gave in briefly to temptation and tipped her chin up,

and placed a kiss on her lips. "There's plenty of hot water still left in the tank," he said softly, stroking her chin. "Go ahead and take a shower before it gets completely dark, and then I'll take one."

He continued to stroke her chin when he added, "Then what I want is for us to do something we should have done months ago, Sienna. I want us to sit down and talk. And I mean to really talk. Regain that level of communication we once had. And what I need to know more than anything is whether my love will ever be just enough for you."

## Chapter 12

*You're my wife. I love you. I will always love you. When we married, we became one.*

Dane's words flowed through Sienna's mind as she stepped into the shower, causing a warm, fuzzy, glowing feeling to seep through her pores. Hope flared within her although she didn't want it to. She hadn't wanted to end her marriage, but when things had begun to get worse between her and Dane, she'd finally decided to take her in-laws' suggestion and get out of their son's life.

Even after three years of seeing how happy she and Dane were together, they still couldn't look beyond her past. They saw her as a nobody, a person who had married their son for his money. She had offered to sign a prenuptial before the wedding and Dane had scoffed at the suggestion, refusing to even draw one up. But still, his parents had made it known each time they saw her just how much they resented the marriage.

And no matter how many times Dane had stood up to them and had put them in their place regarding her, it would only be a matter of time before they resorted to their old ways again, though never in the presence of their son. Maybe Dane was right, and all she'd had to do was tell his parents off once and for all and that would be the end of it, but she never could find the courage to do it.

And what was so hilarious with the entire situation was that she had basically become a workaholic to become successful in her own right so they could see her as their son's equal in every way; and in trying to impress them she had alienated Dane to the point that eventually he would have gotten fed up and asked her for a divorce if she hadn't done so first.

After spending time under the spray of water, she stepped out of the shower, intent on making sure there was enough hot water left for Dane. She tried to put out of her mind the last time she had taken a shower in this stall, and how Dane had joined her in it.

Toweling off, she was grateful she still had some of her belongings at the cabin to sleep in. The last thing she needed was to parade around Dane half naked. Then they would never get any talking done.

She slipped into a T-shirt and a pair of sweatpants she found in one of the drawers. Dane wanted to talk. How could they have honest communication without getting into a discussion about his parents again? She crossed her arms, trying to ignore the chill she was beginning to feel in the air. In order to stay warm they would probably both have to sleep in front of the fireplace tonight. She didn't want to think about what the possibility of doing something like that meant.

While her cell phone still had life, she decided to let her best friend, Vanessa Steele, know that she wouldn't be returning to Charlotte tonight. Dane was right. Not everyone with money acted like his parents. The Steeles, owners of a huge manufacturing company in Charlotte, were just as wealthy as the Bradfords. But they were as down-to-earth as people could get, which proved that not everyone with a lot of money were snobs.

"Hello?"

"Van, it's Sienna."

"Sienna, I was just thinking about you. Did you make it back before that snowstorm hit?"

"No, I'm in the mountains, stranded."

"What! Do you want me to send my cousins to rescue you?"

Sienna smiled. Vanessa was talking about her four single male cousins, Chance, Sebastian, Morgan and Donovan Steele. Sienna had to admit that besides being handsome as sin, they were dependable to a fault. And of all people, she, Vanessa and Vanessa's two younger sisters, Taylor and Cheyenne, should know more than anyone since they had been notorious for getting into trouble while growing up and the brothers four had always been there to bail them out.

"No, I don't need your cousins to come and rescue me."

"What about Dane? You know how I feel about you divorcing him, Sienna. He's still legally your husband and I think I should let him know where you are and let him decide if he should—"

"Vanessa," Sienna interrupted. "You don't have to let Dane know anything. He's here, stranded with me."

## Chapter 13

"How was your shower?" Dane asked Sienna when she returned to the living room a short while later.

"Great. Now it's your turn to indulge."

"Okay." Dane tried not to notice how the candlelight was flickering over Sienna's features, giving them an ethereal glow. He shoved his hands into the pockets of his jeans and for a long moment he stood there staring at her.

She lifted a brow. "What's wrong?"

"I was just thinking how incredibly beautiful you are."

Sienna breathed in deeply, trying to ignore the rush of sensations she felt from his words. "Thank you." Dane had always been a man who'd been free with his compliments. Being apart from him made her realize that was one of the things she missed, among many others.

"I'll be back in a little while," he said before leaving the room.

When he was gone, Sienna remembered the conversation she'd had with Vanessa earlier. Her best friend saw her and Dane being stranded together on the mountain as a twist of fate that Sienna should use to her advantage. Vanessa further thought that for once, Sienna should stand up to the elder Bradfords and not struggle to prove herself to them. Dane had accepted her as she was and now it was time for her to be satisfied and happy with that; after all, she wasn't married to his parents.

A part of Sienna knew that Vanessa was right, but she had been seeking love from others for so long that she hadn't been able to accept that Dane's love was all the love she needed. Before her shower he had asked if his love was enough and now she knew that it was. It was past time for her to acknowledge that fact and to let him know it.

Dane stepped out the shower and began toweling off. The bathroom carried Sienna's scent and the honeysuckle fragrance of the shower gel she enjoyed using.

Given their situation, he really should be worried what they would be faced with if the weather didn't let up in a couple of days with the little bit of food they had. But for now the thought of being stranded here with Sienna overrode all his concerns about that. In his heart, he truly believed they would manage to get through any given situation. Now he had the task of convincing her of that.

He glanced down at his left hand and studied his wedding band. Two weeks ago when he had come here for his pity party, he had taken it off in anger and thrown it in a drawer. It was only when he had returned to Charlotte that he realized he'd left it here in the cabin. At first he had shrugged it off as having no significant meaning since he would be a divorced man in a month's time anyway, but every day he'd felt that a part of him was missing.

In addition to reminding him of Sienna's absence from his life, to Dane, his ring signified their love and the vows that they had made, and a part of him refused to give that up. That's what had driven him back here this weekend—to reclaim the one element of his marriage that he refused to part with yet. Something he felt was rightfully his.

It seemed his ring wasn't the only thing that was rightfully his that he would get the chance to reclaim. More than anything, he wanted his wife back.

# Chapter 14

Dane walked into the living room and stopped in his tracks. Sienna sat in front of the fireplace, cross-legged, with a tray of cookies and two glasses of wine. He knew where the cookies had come from, but where the heck had she gotten the wine?

She must have heard him because she glanced over his way and smiled. At that moment he thought she was even more breathtaking than a rose in winter. She licked her lips and immediately he thought she was even more tempting than any decadent dessert.

He cleared his throat. "Where did the wine come from?"

She licked her lips again and his body responded in an unquestionable way. He hoped the candlelight was hiding the physical effect she was having on him. "I found it in one of the kitchen cabinets. I think it's the bottle that was left when we came here to celebrate our first anniversary."

His thoughts immediately remembered that weekend. She had packed a selection of sexy lingerie and he had enjoyed removing each and every piece. She had also given him, among other things, a beautiful gold watch with the inscription engraved, *The Great Dane*. He, in turn, had given her a lover's bracelet, which was similar to a diamond tennis bracelet except that each letter of her name was etched in six of the stones.

He could still remember the single tear that had fallen from her eye when he had placed it on her wrist. That had been a special time for them, memories he would always cherish. That knowledge tightened the love that surrounded his heart. More than anything, he was determined that they settle things this weekend. He needed to make her see that he was hers and she was his. For always.

His lips creased into a smile. "I see you've decided to share the cookies, after all," he said, crossing the room to her.

She chuckled as he dropped down on the floor beside her. "Either that or run the risk of you getting up during the night and eating them all." The firelight danced through the twists on her head, highlighting the medium brown coiled strands with golden flecks. He absolutely loved the natural looking hairstyle on her.

He lifted a dark brow. "Eating them all? Three boxes?"

Her smile grew soft. "Hey, you've been known to over-indulge a few times."

He paused as heated memories consumed him, reminding him of those times he had overindulged, especially when it came to making love to her. He recalled one weekend they had gone at it almost nonstop. If she hadn't been on the pill there was no doubt in his mind that that single weekend would have made him a daddy. A very proud one, at that.

She handed him a glass of wine. "May I propose a toast?"

His smile widened. "To what?"

"The return of the Beast from the East."

He switched his gaze from her to glance out the window. Even in the dark he could see the white flecks coming down in droves. He looked back at her and cocked a brow. "We have a reason to celebrate this bad weather?"

She stared at him for a long moment, then said quietly, "Yes. The Beast is the reason we're stranded here together, and even with our low rations of food, I can't think of any other place I'd rather be…than here alone with you."

## Chapter 15

Dane stared at Sienna and the intensity of that gaze made her entire body tingle, her nerve endings steam. It was pretty much like the day they'd met, when he'd walked into his father's study. She had looked up, their gazes had connected and the seriousness in the dark irises that had locked with hers had changed her life forever. She had fallen in love with him then and there.

Dane didn't say anything for a long moment as he continued to look at her, and then he lifted his wineglass and said huskily, "To the Beast…who brought me Beauty."

His words were like a sensuous stroke down her spine, and the void feeling she'd had during the past few months was slowly fading away. After the toast was made and they had both taken sips of their wine, Dane placed his glass aside and then relieved her of hers. He then slowly leaned forward and captured her mouth, tasting the wine, relishing her delectable flavor. How had she gone without this for six months? How had she survived? she wondered as his tongue devoured hers, battering deep in the heat of her mouth, licking and sucking as he wove his tongue in and out between teeth, gum and whatever wanted to serve as a barrier.

He suddenly pulled back and stared at her. A smile touched the corners of his lips. "I could keep going and going, but before we go any further we need to talk, determine what brought us to this point so it won't ever be allowed to happen again. I don't want us to ever let anything or anyone have power, more control over the vows we made three years ago."

Sienna nodded, thinking the way the firelight was dancing over his dark skin was sending an erotic frisson up her spine. "All right."

He stood. "I'll be right back."

Sienna lifted a brow, wondering where he was going and watched as he crossed the room to open the desk drawer. Like her, he had changed into a T-shirt and a pair of sweats, and as she watched him she found it difficult to breathe. He moved in such a manly way, each movement a display of fine muscles and limbs and how they worked together in graceful coordination, perfect precision. Watching him only knocked her hormones out of whack.

He returned moments later with pens and paper in hand. There was a serious expression on his face when he handed her a sheet of paper and a pen and kept the same for himself. "I want us to write down all the things we feel went wrong with our marriage, being honest to include everything. And then we'll discuss them."

She looked down at the pen and paper and then back at him. "You want me to write them down?"

"Yes, and I'll do the same."

Sienna nodded and watched as he began writing on his paper, wondering what he was jotting down. She leaned back and sighed, wondering if she could air their dirty laundry on paper, but it seemed he had no such qualms. Most couples sought the helpful guidance of marriage counselors when they found themselves in similar situations, but she hadn't given them that chance. But at this point, she would do anything to save her marriage.

So she began writing, being honest with herself and with him.

## Chapter 16

Dane finished writing and glanced over at Sienna. She was still at it and had a serious expression on her features. He studied the contours of her face and his gaze dropped to her neck, and he noticed the thin gold chain. She was still wearing the heart pendant he'd given her as a wedding gift.

Deep down, Dane believed this little assignment was what they needed as the first step in repairing what had gone wrong in their marriage. Having things written down would make it easier to stay focused and not go off on a tangent. And it made one less likely to give in to the power of the mind, the wills and emotions. He wanted them to concentrate on those destructive elements and forces that had eroded away at what should have been a strong relationship.

She glanced up and met his gaze as she put the pen aside. She gave him a wry smile. "Okay, that's it."

He reached out and took her hand in his, tightening his hold on it when he saw a look of uncertainty on her face. "All right, what do you have?"

She gave him a sheepish grimace. "How about you going first?"

He gently squeezed her hand. "How about if we go together? I'll start off and then we'll alternate."

She nodded. "What if we have the same ones?"

"That will be okay. We'll talk about all of them." He picked up his piece of paper.

"First on my list is communication."

Sienna smiled ruefully. "It's first on mine, too. And I agree that we need to talk more, without arguing, not that you argued. I think you would hold stuff in when I made you upset instead of getting it out and speaking your mind."

Dane stared at her for a moment, then a smile touched his lips. "You're right, you know. I always had to plug in the last word and I did it because I knew it would piss you off."

"Well, stop doing it."

He grinned. "Okay. The next time I'll hang around for us to talk through things. But then you're going to have to make sure that you're available when we need to talk. You can't let anything, not even your job, get in the way of us communicating."

"Okay, I agree."

"Now, what's next on your list?" he asked.

She looked up at him and smiled. "Patience. I know you said that I don't have patience, but neither do you. But you used to."

Dane shook his head. "Yeah, I lost my patience when you did. I thought to myself, why should I be patient with you when you weren't doing the same with me? Sometimes I think you thought I enjoyed knowing you had a bad day or didn't make a sale, and that wasn't it at all. At some point what was suddenly important to you wasn't important to me anymore."

"And because of it, we both became detached," Sienna said softly.

"Yes, we did." He reached out and lifted her chin. "I promise to do a better job of being patient, Sienna."

"So will I, Dane."

They alternated, going down the list. They had a number of the same things on both lists and they discussed everything in detail, acknowledging their faults and what they could have done to make things better. They also discussed what they would do in the future to strengthen their marriage.

"That's all I have on my list," Dane said a while later. "Do you have anything else?"

Sienna's finger glided over her list. For a short while she thought about pretending she didn't have anything else, but they had agreed to be completely honest. They had definitely done so when they had discussed her spending more time at work than at home.

"So what's the last thing on your list, Sienna? What do you see as one of the things that went wrong with our marriage?"

She lifted her chin and met his gaze and said, "My inability to stand up to your parents."

He looked at her with deep, dark eyes. "Okay, then. Let's talk about that."

# Chapter 17

Dane waited patiently for Sienna to begin talking and gently rubbed the backside of her hand while doing so. He'd known the issue of his parents had always been a challenge to her. Over the years, he had tried to make her see that how the elder Bradfords felt didn't matter. What he failed to realize, accept and understand was that it *did* matter…to her.

She had grown up in a family without love for so long that when they married, she not only sought his love, but that of his family. Being accepted meant a lot to her, and her expectations of the Bradfords, given how they operated and their family history, were too high.

They weren't a close-knit bunch, never had been and never would be. His parents had allowed their own parents to decide their future, including who they married. When they had come of age, arranged marriages were the norm within the Bradfords' circle. His father had once confided to him one night after indulging in too many drinks that his mother had not been his choice for a wife. That hadn't surprised Dane, nor had it bothered him, since he would bet that his father probably hadn't been his mother's choice of a husband, either.

"I don't want to rehash the past, Dane," Sienna finally said softly, looking at the blaze in the fireplace instead of at him. "But something you said earlier tonight has made me think about a lot of things. You love your parents, but you've never hesitated in letting them know when you felt they were wrong, nor have you put up with their crap when it came to me."

She switched her gaze from the fire to him. "The problem is that *I* put up with their crap when it came to me. And you were right. I thought I had to actually prove something to them, show them I was worthy of you and your love. And I've spent the better part of a year and a half doing that and all it did was bring me closer and closer to losing you. I'm sure they've been walking around with big smiles on their faces since you got the divorce petition. But I refuse to let them be happy at my expense and my own heartbreak."

She scooted closer to Dane and splayed her hands against his chest. "It's time I became more assertive with your parents, Dane. Because it's not about them—it's about us. I refuse to let them make me feel unworthy any longer, because I am worthy to be loved by you. I don't have anything to prove. They either accept me as I am or not at all. The only person who matters anymore is you."

With his gaze holding hers, Dane lifted one of her hands off his chest and brought it to his lips, and placed a kiss on the palm. "I'm glad you've finally come to realize that, Sienna. And I wholeheartedly understand and agree. I was made to love you, and if my parents never accept that then it's their loss, not ours."

Tears constricted Sienna's throat and she swallowed deeply before she could find her voice to say, "I love you, Dane. I don't want the divorce. I never did. I want to belong to you and I want you to belong to me. I just want to make you happy."

"And I love you, too, Sienna, and I don't want the divorce, either. My life will be nothing without you being a part of it. I love you so much and I've missed you."

And with his heart pounding hard in his chest, he leaned over and captured her lips, intent on showing her just what he meant.

# Chapter 18

*This is homecoming*, Sienna thought as she was quickly consumed by the hungry onslaught of Dane's kiss. All the hurt and anger she'd felt for six months was being replaced by passion of the most heated kind. All she could think about was the desire she was feeling being back in the arms of the man she loved and who loved her.

This was the type of communication she'd always loved, where she could share her thoughts, feelings and desires with Dane without uttering a single word. It was where their deepest emotions and what was in their inner hearts spoke for them, expressing things so eloquently and not leaving any room for misunderstandings.

He pulled back slightly, his lips hovering within inches of hers. He reached out and caressed her cheek, and as if she needed his taste again, her lips automatically parted. A slow, sensual acknowledgment of understanding tilted the corners of his mouth into a smile. Then he leaned closer and kissed her again, longer and harder, and the only thing she could do was to wrap her arms around him and silently thank God for reuniting her with this very special man.

Dane was hungry for the taste of his wife and at that moment, as his heart continued to pound relentlessly in his chest, he knew he had to make love to her, to show her in every way what she meant to him, had always meant to him and would always mean to him.

He pulled back slightly and the moisture that was left on her lips made his stomach clench. He leaned forward and licked them dry, or tried to, but her scent was driving him to do more. "Please let me make love to you, Sienna," he whispered, leaning down and resting his forehead against hers.

She leaned back and cupped his chin with her hand. "Oh, yes. I want you to make love to me, Dane. I've missed being with you so much I ache."

"Oh, baby, I love you." He pulled her closer, murmured the words in her twisted locks, kissed her cheek, her temple, her lips, and he cupped her buttocks, practically lifting her off the floor in the process. His breath came out harsh, ragged, as the chemistry between them sizzled. There was only one way to drench their fire.

He stretched out with her in front of the fireplace as he began removing her clothes and then his. Moments later, the blaze from the fire was a flickering light across their naked skin. And then he began kissing her all over, leaving no part of her untouched, determined to quench his hunger and his desire. He had missed the taste of her and was determined to be reacquainted in every way he could think of.

"Dane…"

Her tortured moan ignited the passion within him and he leaned forward to position his body over hers, letting his throbbing erection come to rest between her thighs, gently touching the entrance of her moist heat. He lifted his head to look down at her, wanting to see her expression the exact moment their bodies joined again.

# *Chapter 19*

Sienna stared into Dane's eyes, the heat and passion she saw in them making her shiver. The love she recognized made her heart pound, and the desire she felt for him sent surges and surges of sensations through every part of her body, especially the area between her legs, making her thighs quiver.

"You're my everything, Sienna," he whispered as he began easing inside of her. His gaze was locked with hers as his voice came out in a husky tone. "I need you like I need air to breathe, water for thirst and food for nourishment. Oh, baby, my life has been so empty since you've been gone. I love and need you."

His words touched her and when he was embedded inside of her to the hilt, she arched her back, needing and wanting even more of him. She gripped his shoulders with her fingers as liquid fire seemed to flow to all parts of her body.

And at that moment she forgot everything—the Beast from the East, their limited supply of food and the fact they were stranded together in a cabin with barely enough heat. The only thing that registered in her mind was that they were together and expressing their love in a way that literally touched her soul.

He continued to stroke her, in and out, and with each powerful thrust into her body she moaned out his name and told him of her love. She was like a bow whose strings were being stretched to the limit each and every time he drove into her, and she met his thrusts with her own eager ones.

And then she felt it, the strength like a volcano erupting as he continued to stroke her to oblivion. Her body splintered into a thousand pieces as an orgasm ripped through her, almost snatching her breath away. And when she felt him buck, tighten his hold on her hips and thrust into her deeper, she knew that same powerful sensation had taken hold of him, as well.

"Sienna!"

He screamed her name and growled a couple of words that were incoherent to her ears. She tightened her arms around his neck, needing to be as close to him as she could get. She knew in her heart at that moment that things were going to be fine. She and Dane had proved that when it came to the power of love, it was never too late.

Sienna awoke the following morning naked, in front of the fireplace and cuddled in her husband's arms with a blanket covering them. After yawning, she raised her chin and glanced over at him and met his gaze head-on. The intensity in the dark eyes staring back at her shot heat through all parts of her body. She couldn't help but recall last night and how they had tried making up for all the time they had been apart.

"It's gone," Dane said softly, pulling her closer into his arms.

She lifted a brow. "What's gone?"

"The Beast."

She tilted her head to glance out the window and he

was right. Although snow was still falling, it wasn't the violent blizzard that had been unleashed the day before. It was as if the weather had served the purpose it had come for and had made its exit. She smiled. Evidently, someone up there knew she and Dane's relationship was meant to be saved and had stepped in to salvage it.

She was about to say something when suddenly there was a loud pounding at the door. She and Dane looked at each other, wondering who would be paying them a visit to the cabin at this hour and in this weather.

# Chapter 20

Sienna, like Dane, had quickly gotten dressed and was now staring at the four men who were standing in the doorway…those handsome Steele brothers. She smiled, shaking her head. Vanessa had evidently called her cousins to come rescue her, anyway.

"Vanessa called us," Chance Steele, the oldest of the pack, said by way of explanation. "It just so happened that we were only a couple of miles down the road at our own cabin." A smile touched his lips. "She was concerned that the two of you were here starving to death and asked us to share some of our rations."

"Thanks, guys," Dane said, gladly accepting the box Sebastian Steele was handing him. "Come on in. And although we've had plenty of heat to keep us warm, I have to admit our food supply was kind of low."

As soon as the four entered, all eyes went to Sienna. Although the brothers knew Dane because their families sometimes ran in the same social circles, as well as the fact that Dane and Donovan Steele had graduated from high school the same year, she knew their main concern was for her. She had been their cousin Vanessa's best friend for years, and as a result they had sort of adopted her as their little cousin, as well.

"You okay?" Morgan Steele asked her, although Sienna knew she had to look fine; probably like a woman who'd been made love to all night, and she wasn't ashamed of that fact. After all, Dane *was* her husband. But the Steeles knew about her pending divorce, so she decided to end their worries.

She smiled and moved closer to Dane. He automatically wrapped his arms around her shoulders and brought her closer to his side. "Yes, I'm wonderful," she said, breaking the subtle tension she felt in the room. "Dane and I have decided we don't want a divorce and intend to stay together and make our marriage work."

The relieved smiles on the faces of the four men were priceless. "That's wonderful. We're happy for you," Donovan Steele said, grinning.

"We apologize if we interrupted anything, but you know Vanessa," Chance said, smiling. "She wouldn't let up. We would have come sooner but the bad weather kept us away."

"Your timing was perfect," Dane said, grinning. "We appreciate you even coming out now. I'm sure the roads weren't their best."

"No, but my new truck managed just fine," Sebastian said proudly. "Besides, we're going fishing later. We would invite you to join us, Dane, but I'm sure you can think of other ways you'd prefer to spend your time."

Dane smiled as he glanced down and met Sienna's gaze. "Oh, yeah, I can definitely think of a few."

The power had been restored and a couple of hours later, after eating a hefty breakfast of pancakes, sausage, grits and eggs, and drinking what Dane had to admit was the best coffee he'd had in a long time, Dane and Sienna were wrapped in each other's arms in the king-size bed. Sensations flowed through her just thinking about how they had ached and hungered for each other, and the fierceness of their lovemaking to fulfill that need and greed.

"Now will you tell me what brought you to the cabin?" Sienna asked, turning in Dane's arms and meeting his gaze.

"My wedding band." He then told her why he'd come to the cabin two weeks ago and how he'd left the ring behind. "It was as if without that ring on my finger, my connection to you was gone. I had to have it back so I came here for it."

Sienna nodded, understanding completely. That was one of the reasons she hadn't removed hers. Reaching out she cupped his stubble jaw in her hand and then leaned over and kissed him softly. "Together forever, Mr. Bradford."

Dane smiled. "Yes, Mrs. Bradford, together forever. We've proved that when it comes to true love, it's never too late."

\* \* \* \* \*

*NEVER TOO LATE is part of*
*Brenda Jackson's*
**FORGED OF STEELE** *series*
*Don't miss the latest story,*

*POSSESSED BY PASSION,*
*Available March 2016*
*from*
*Kimani Romance.*

*And be sure to*
*pick up the other*
*stories in*
**FORGED OF STEELE:**

*SOLID SOUL*
*NIGHT HEAT*
*BEYOND TEMPTATION*
*RISKY PLEASURES*
*IRRESISTIBLE FORCES*
*INTIMATE SEDUCTION*
*HIDDEN PLEASURES*
*A STEELE FOR CHRISTMAS*
*PRIVATE ARRANGEMENTS*

*Available from Kimani Romance.*

# COMING NEXT MONTH FROM

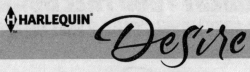
## HARLEQUIN® *Desire*

### Available March 1, 2016

## #2431 THE CEO'S UNEXPECTED CHILD
*Billionaires and Babies* • by Andrea Laurence
When a fertility clinic makes a mistake, a recent widow discovers her infant daughter doesn't belong to her late husband, but to a billionaire set on claiming his new family...by any means.

## #2432 THE SEAL'S SECRET HEIRS
*Texas Cattleman's Club: Lies and Lullabies*
by Kat Cantrell
A former Navy SEAL comes home to his greatest challenge yet—surprise fatherhood of secret twins—only to discover his high school sweetheart is his children's social worker. Will the first-time father get a second shot at real love?

## #2433 SNOWBOUND WITH THE BOSS
*Pregnant by the Boss* • by Maureen Child
When gaming tycoon Sean Ryan is stranded with irascible, irresistible contractor Kate Wells, the temptation to keep each other warm proves overwhelming. Dealing with unexpected feelings is hard enough, but what about an unexpected pregnancy? They're about to find out...

## #2434 ONE SECRET NIGHT, ONE SECRET BABY
*Moonlight Beach Bachelors* • by Charlene Sands
Though Hollywood heartthrob Dylan McKay has no memory of that fateful night with his sister's best friend, he must face the music. He's made her pregnant and will make her his bride. But soon the shocking, unforgettable truth emerges...

## #2435 THE RANCHER'S MARRIAGE PACT
*Texas Extreme* • by Kristi Gold
Marrying his sexy interior designer is convenient enough for rich rancher Dallas Calloway. He'll get his inheritance and she'll get a new lease on life. Then the business arrangement turns into more than they bargain for...

## #2436 HIS SECRETARY'S SURPRISE FIANCÉ
*Bayou Billionaires* • by Joanne Rock
Winning at any cost might work on the football field, but will demanding a fake engagement really keep billionaire sportsman Dempsey Reynaud's alluring assistant in his life?

———————

# REQUEST YOUR FREE BOOKS!
## 2 FREE NOVELS PLUS 2 FREE GIFTS!

**H HARLEQUIN®**

*Desire*

## ALWAYS POWERFUL, PASSIONATE AND PROVOCATIVE

**YES!** Please send me 2 FREE Harlequin® Desire novels and my 2 FREE gifts (gifts are worth about $10). After receiving them, if I don't wish to receive any more books, I can return the shipping statement marked "cancel." If I don't cancel, I will receive 6 brand-new novels every month and be billed just $4.55 per book in the U.S. or $5.24 per book in Canada. That's a savings of at least 13% off the cover price! It's quite a bargain! Shipping and handling is just 50¢ per book in the U.S. and 75¢ per book in Canada.* I understand that accepting the 2 free books and gifts places me under no obligation to buy anything. I can always return a shipment and cancel at any time. Even if I never buy another book, the two free books and gifts are mine to keep forever.

225/326 HDN GH2P

Name _____ (PLEASE PRINT)

Address _____ Apt. #

City _____ State/Prov. _____ Zip/Postal Code

Signature (if under 18, a parent or guardian must sign)

### Mail to the **Reader Service:**
**IN U.S.A.:** P.O. Box 1867, Buffalo, NY 14240-1867
**IN CANADA:** P.O. Box 609, Fort Erie, Ontario L2A 5X3

**Want to try two free books from another line?**
**Call 1-800-873-8635 or visit www.ReaderService.com.**

* Terms and prices subject to change without notice. Prices do not include applicable taxes. Sales tax applicable in N.Y. Canadian residents will be charged applicable taxes. Offer not valid in Quebec. This offer is limited to one order per household. Not valid for current subscribers to Harlequin Desire books. All orders subject to credit approval. Credit or debit balances in a customer's account(s) may be offset by any other outstanding balance owed by or to the customer. Please allow 4 to 6 weeks for delivery. Offer available while quantities last.

**Your Privacy**—The Reader Service is committed to protecting your privacy. Our Privacy Policy is available online at www.ReaderService.com or upon request from the Reader Service.

We make a portion of our mailing list available to reputable third parties that offer products we believe may interest you. If you prefer that we not exchange your name with third parties, or if you wish to clarify or modify your communication preferences, please visit us at www.ReaderService.com/consumerchoice or write to us at Reader Service Preference Service, P.O. Box 9062, Buffalo, NY 14240-9062. Include your complete name and address.

HD15

Claire looked completely panicked by the thought of Luca having access to her child.

Their child.

It seemed so wrong for him to have a child with a woman he'd never met. But now that he had a living, breathing daughter, he wasn't about to sit back and pretend it didn't happen. Eva was probably the only child he would ever have, and he'd already missed months of her life. That would not continue.

"We can and we will." Luca spoke up at last. "Eva is my daughter, and I've got the paternity test results to prove it. There's not a judge in the county of New York who won't grant me emergency visitation while we await our court date. They will say when and where and how often you have to give her to me."

Claire sat, her mouth agape at his words. "She's just a baby. She's only six months old. Why fight me for her just so you can hand her over to a nanny?"

Luca laughed at her presumptuous tone. "What makes you so certain I'll have a nanny for her?"

"You're a rich, powerful, unmarried businessman. You're better suited to run a corporation than to change a diaper. I'm willing to bet you don't have the first clue of how to care for an infant, much less the time."

Luca just shook his head and sat forward in his seat. "You know very little about me, *tesorino*, you've said so yourself, so don't presume anything about me."

Claire narrowed her gaze at him. She definitely didn't like him pushing her. And he was pushing her. Partially because he liked to see the fire in her eyes and the flush of her skin, and partially because it was necessary to get through to her.

Neither of them had asked for this to happen to them, but she needed to learn she wasn't in charge. They had to cooperate if this awkward situation was going to improve. He'd started off nice, politely requesting to see Eva, and he'd been flatly ignored. As each request was met with silence, he'd escalated the pressure. That's how they'd ended up here today. If she pushed him any further, he would start playing hardball. He didn't want to, but he would crush her like his restaurants' competitors.

"We can work together and play nice, or my lawyer here can make things very difficult for you. As he said, it's your choice."

"What are you suggesting, Mr. Moretti?" her lawyer asked.

"I'm suggesting we both take a little time away from our jobs and spend it together."

*Don't miss*
*THE CEO'S UNEXPECTED CHILD*
*by Andrea Laurence, available March 2016 wherever*
*Harlequin® Desire books and ebooks are sold.*

www.Harlequin.com